# between the lines

## ACROSS THE YEARS, BOOK 2

### SARA R. TURNQUIST

MOUNTAIN
SUMMIT PRESS

*If you would like to stay up-to-date on this and other series from Sara and receive a free ebook, sign up for her newsletter:*

https://saraturnquist.com/list

*For everyone who fights animosity*
*and refuses to let anything steal their faith.*

# ONE

## *a new beginning*

*February 17, 2020*
*Cherry Lane Inn*
*Murfreesboro, TN*

What did one look for in a place to get married? Brianne Marshall let out a breath. She didn't want to make it such an all-important decision, but it was. To her. Scott seemed quite a bit more laid back. Sometimes that read as a lack of care. But she wanted to believe that she was wrong. She told herself as much. Several times over the last few months.

But they were getting married. After everything, Scott stayed by her side. Through the depression, the recovery, the highs and lows...everything. She couldn't be happier to be marrying him in just four short months. June seemed so far away, but right around the corner.

"The chairs will line up here," the tall woman said, indicating one side of the room.

Everything about the event space coordinator was long and lean. And she smiled a little too readily at Scott. It dug at Brianne a little. When she turned to Scott, the way his eyes gleamed when he met Brianne's gaze, she knew she had found a man who treasured her. That's what she needed.

"What instruments were you thinking you would need? We have space in that corner." The woman pointed a perfectly manicured hand.

"We thought a pianist. And a singer. Right?" Scott turned his brown eyes on her again.

She nodded. "Unless you thought we would need more?" After all, Scott was the musician. But she had kind of always dreamed of a simple wedding.

He reached for her hand. "I like the idea of the pianist and singer. It's easy. And uncluttered."

Brianne smiled in spite of herself and squeezed his hand, which warmed more than her fingers.

The coordinator smiled sweetly before looking at her clipboard. "I think that's all I needed. Do you two have any questions?" She spoke to them both, but it seemed her gaze settled on Scott alone.

Because he was easy to look at...he certainly was that. Or because the woman didn't think Brianne's opinion mattered?

Goodness! she chided herself. What has this woman done to deserve such judgment? Nothing.

Brianne refocused on Scott, who was shaking his head. "Nothing I can think of." He tugged on Brianne's hand, bringing her a little closer to himself. "You?"

Disentangling herself from Scott's hold, she flipped open her binder and thumbed to the section on venue. She scanned the page, but everything seemed to blur right before her. It may be time to call it a day. Closing the wedding binder and hugging it to herself, she shook her head.

"Well, if you think of anything, please call or email. You have my information?"

"Yes," Brianne was quick to say. She had compiled the pertinent contacts early on.

Scott moved closer to her and set a hand to her back.

She loved that he kept contact with her, but her nerves plagued her around this woman who apparently had no flaws.

"Then I think we're done here." There was that perfect white smile flashing at them.

Then the coordinator turned and moved toward the front of the building.

Scott pressed gently against the small of Brianne's back and urged her forward as well. He leaned in and whispered, "You okay?"

This was no time for such a question. Not in front of this woman. Brianne tensed.

He rubbed his hand in a small circle but said nothing further. Perhaps he was weary of reassuring her.

As the coordinator reached for the door knob, she paused then turned. "Oh, there is one more thing."

Brianne had to stop abruptly to keep from bumping into her. But Scott's hand on her arm helped her retain her balance.

"What's that?" Scott asked. Though his eyes were on Brianne, eyebrows raised. Did he have to be so concerned? She hated being a source of worry.

"Due to...the unfortunate circumstances in our world right now," the woman was slow to say. It was as if she really didn't want to. "...we are having to talk to all of our couples about contingencies."

"Contingencies?" Scott's brow furrowed.

What could the coordinator be referring to? Then, it rushed through Brianne. The corona-sars virus. A shiver went down her spine.

Scott rubbed a hand up her back and to her shoulder, giving it a squeeze. Again, he was reassuring her.

And perhaps it was necessary. This virus moving across the world, and even into the Unites States earlier this month despite travel bans, had Brianne wanting to run to the hills. But there was no guarantee she'd be safe there. Or anywhere. Oddly, that was the thing that kept her grounded and still in Memphis. That, and Scott's insistence that it was much ado about nothing. The media exaggerates, he would say...they need to sensationalize for their story.

The coordinator had continued talking. How had Brianne spaced out? But she tried her best to focus. The anchor in her gut and rush of apprehension through her body didn't help matters.

"We just need to have a plan. It's not likely we will need it." The woman waved a hand in the air. "But it's best to have it."

"We will discuss it," Scott said, swallowing hard. Was he upset the coordinator brought it up? Or at Brianne's reaction? "And get back to you."

"That will be fine." There was that smile again. "If you could do so by the end of the week, that will help us solidify things."

"Sure thing." Scott looked at Brianne.

She attempted a smile, though it felt uneven, and nodded. "Of course."

"Are you headed back today? Or plan to enjoy the area?" The woman led them outside and toward the parking lot. Why did she ask that? Making small talk? Or overly curious?

"We plan to check out the Italian restaurant in downtown. We're not from Murfreesboro, so we are narrowing down where we want to have the rehearsal dinner."

"That is a wonderful place!" Again, the beaming smile. "I hope you have a fantastic meal."

"Then I think we'll stay the night in Clarksville and head back to Memphis tomorrow."

"Y'all are superstars...planning a wedding so far from your location. People do it, but it requires a lot of organization."

Scott's smile spread across his face and he tugged Brianne closer. "Brianne has that in spades. You have seen the binder, right?"

Wait. Was he teasing her?

"I have." The woman's laugh seemed uneasy.

Or maybe Brianne was still being judgmental. Perhaps unnecessarily.

"Have a great lunch. And we'll touch base soon?" Again, she looked at Scott. Was she so averse to communication with Brianne? Or did she wish for more of the exchanges to be with Scott? It was difficult to discern. And Brianne was tired of second guessing everything.

The woman turned and walked back to the building, leaving them alone by Scott's car.

Brianne moved toward the passenger side door.

Scott was close behind, reaching for the handle. But as he opened the door, he paused. "You didn't answer me. Is something bothering you?"

She shrugged, not wanting to have this conversation. They'd had it before, and as understanding as Scott was, she felt like a heel the whole time. "It's nothing."

He lifted his eyebrows and set hands to her shoulders, steering her to face him. "Really? It doesn't seem like nothing."

She shook her head. "It's just all the planning. And this stuff about that virus." Brianne leaned back against the car. "It worries me."

"I know it does, honey. But we won't gain anything but headaches from trying to figure it out. Remember," he said as he let his hands run down her arms and cover her hands, still on her binder, "God's got this. Nothing about any of this surprises Him."

"That's true. But," she started, then stopped herself.

"But what?"

She bit at her lip then decided it was best to be honest with him. "How do we know God's plan doesn't involve hard things? He promises to be with us, but He never promises things won't be hard, or there won't be loss, or—"

Scott pulled her to himself, wrapping his arms around her. "It's okay."

"Is it?" She sniffled as she leaned into him.

All of a sudden, her binder was in the way.

He slipped it from her grasp and set it on the hood of the car. "Yes, it is. Because, whether bad things happen, or we face hard things...His grace is sufficient, and His plan is perfect."

She nodded into his shoulder and closed her eyes, wishing she could believe that as strongly as he did.

The three-hour drive from Clarksville to Memphis had dragged on. Surely it had been longer, Scott thought as he considered how the silence had stretched, becoming thick in the air.

It bothered because he and Brianne did not have such silences between them. Four years together, and they had not run out of things to say. Was she mad? At him? He had no clue. Would it be worse for him if he asked? Was he supposed to know what he had done?

He glanced at Brianne but only saw her profile. She stared out the window as if keenly interested in something on the horizon. What was there that she hadn't seen a million times on this drive?

Swallowing against his trepidation, he reached a hand out and covered hers.

She laced her fingers through his.

There was that. He let out a sigh. Too late, realizing it was probably audible. His gaze flew to her, but she didn't seem to notice anything. A blessing for certain.

Resisting the urge to squeeze her hand, he cleared his throat. "Hey," he said, careful to keep his tone soft. "We don't have to go to my parents' house for dinner. We can hit up Dixie Cafe. Get some comfort food."

Her gaze was on him then. He felt it. Glancing briefly, he attempted to gauge her mood. But her face was a mask. Except her eyes...they seemed all the more deep in that moment in a way that made him want to pull her closer and soothe her aches.

"Do you not want to eat with your folks?" Her words belied a confusion that surprised him. He thought his intentions were clear.

"No, that's not it. I just didn't know if you needed some time for just us." He squeezed her hand gently. "Or maybe just want me to take you to your apartment?" Though he offered it, he prayed that was not what she opted for.

She shifted in the passenger seat, angling toward him. "It almost sounds as if you'd rather I just go to the apartment."

Great. He'd found himself in a trap. "No, Brie, that's not it. I just...I want you to have options. I want you to be comfortable."

She turned her focus back to the road. The silence even worse than before.

"I'm not saying any of this right," he grumbled. "I'm sorry."

She rubbed a thumb across his hand. It was the sweetest reassurance she could have given him.

"You've been..." He wanted to say *off*. The word was on the tip of his tongue before he caught it. That would not come out well. "...distracted."

She murmured something then shifted to look at him again, bringing her other hand around to enfold his from both sides. "You're right. And I'm sorry."

His nerves settled. "What's on your mind?"

For a moment, there was nothing forthcoming. He feared she wasn't going to answer. But then she spoke.

"I...just have a lot I'm thinking through."

"Worried?" He probed where he might shouldn't. But since her breakdown a few years back and the diagnosis of her mood disorder, he wanted to address the reality head on. No way was he going to let that rear its ugly head. Not if he could prevent it.

"Yeah," she said, looking down at their hands. The word was barely a whisper.

"Want to talk about it?"

She seemed to consider his words then shook her head. "I'm not sure what I think yet. I just need some more time to process some things."

Now that surprised him. She usually processed out loud. What weighed on her? As if he didn't know. The wedding. The COVID virus. All of it. Could he blame her?

He brought her hands to his lips and pressed a kiss to the one on top. "You know I'm here when you are ready."

She nodded.

"And, really, we can skip my parents' house. They'll understand. It's been a long weekend."

"No," she said, shaking her curled locks. "I want to go."

He smiled. "Good." Then he shifted and took the car out of cruise control. "Cause we're coming into Arlington."

After kissing her hand again, he released it so he could have both of his hands to steer. They would be at their exit soon.

Sure enough, only a couple of minutes later, the Bartlett exit shone despite the darkening sky. The sun was setting and a burst of oranges and purples filled his vision.

He turned onto the exit, pulling off I-40 west. They'd had their fill of that interstate for some time. Though they'd likely be back, eastbound toward Middle Tennessee. A wedding in Murfreesboro was not his first choice, but he did like the venue they selected. And Brianne had wanted to be closer to her home-town. That was more important than his preference to plan the ceremony to be local to where they both lived.

The familiar streets of Bartlett passed him by as he headed toward the two-story brick house he had called home the longest. His parents had moved around a bit but settled in their current house years ago when his dad opened a counseling practice in nearby Cordova.

In less than ten minutes, Scott turned into his parents' drive-way. He set the car in park and took a deep breath.

"You okay?" Brianne asked the question he had earlier voiced.

He set his gaze on her worried features. "Just worn out from the drive."

"Ah." Then she looked away.

"It's fine," he was quick to say. "I just need to collect myself."

She attempted a smile, but it was slight. And her eyes didn't reflect the levity of the action. Indeed, there was a weight on her mind. Could he coax it out of her? Surely she'd feel better if she talked about it.

But he didn't want to push. So he offered her a smile and said, "Ready?"

She nodded. "As much as I'll ever be."

There was a lightness to her tone, as if this was intended to be a joke. But Scott wondered if there was truth behind it. She still wasn't completely comfortable with his parents. He wasn't blind...he could see it. His mother and Brie both had big personal-ities. And he prayed they would find a rhythm to their rela-tionship.

He opened his door and rushed around to the passenger side; however, she was already halfway out of the car. That wasn't like her. She knew he enjoyed helping her out. Was this a message?

Shaking his head, he opted not to read too much into her action. It would be clearer once she was ready to talk.

He held out his hand and she slid her fingers into it. Giving her a little tug, he drew her closer to his side as they walked to the front door.

His mother was there before he could ring the doorbell.

"Scott, Brianne, so glad you got here safely. You can't know how I worry when you're on that drive." She rushed them inside the house.

The smell of apple pie assaulted him. Of course she would make his favorite. He should expect nothing less.

"I am twenty-five, Mom. I think you can give me some credit."

She waved a hand. "It's my job to worry."

Then she turned and moved toward the living room.

"Please, come in, have a seat."

Something in her manner was almost giddy. What was going on here? He offered Brianne an apologetic shrug. They would soon find out what was behind his mother's behavior. He was certain of it.

He held out a hand for Brianne to settle on the couch. Then he sat beside her and wrapped an arm around her. The little touches in the car had been nice, but he craved more connection with her. Not just pulling her closer to his side but to be on the same page emotionally. He wasn't sure they were lately.

She hesitated to let him tug her closer. But only a little. Her gaze shot to his mother. Did she think his mother disapproved of the action? Not that it mattered to Scott. He wished Bri wouldn't be so anxious about what others thought, for her own sake.

Mother sat in the nearby armchair. Only then did he notice a shoebox sat on the side table. It was out of place. And nothing in his mom's world was ever out of place. Or so it always seemed.

"How was the trip?" she asked, practically bursting with energy. Or a secret.

"It was fine. Nothing eventful."

"Well, that's good. How was your time in Murfreesboro?"

There was a crease forming in Mother's forehead. Scott had already guessed his mother wasn't excited about the wedding location choice.

"Good," he said as he looked at Brie. "Our venue has all the options we wanted. Now, we just need to keep the lines of communication open until the wedding." He squeezed Brie's shoulder at that mention of their special day.

Brianne plastered on a smile and nodded along.

He almost pressed out about the need for a contingency. But he sensed that it would be best he and Brie talk about that before he included his mother's opinion. This was all such a minefield.

"Mom, you look as if you might burst."

"I found something for you." She beamed.

"Found something for me?"

"Yes, I was going through some of the things in the storage closet, clearing stuff out. And I found this." She set a hand on the shoebox.

Scott had a couple of questions. Why was she clearing things out? And what was in the box? Something from his childhood perhaps? He settled on the more curious thing. "What's that?"

Mom pulled the box into her lap then held it out to him.

He took it, taking his arm off the back of the couch.

"Open it." She appeared ready to jump at him if he didn't comply.

Looking toward Brie, he saw that she was rather curious. More so than he was. Interesting. Then he lifted the lid.

Old discolored, slightly tattered envelopes wrapped in ribbon lay within.

He met his mom's gaze "What are these?"

She moved over to the couch to sit next to him.

He and Brianne had to scoot to make room.

"These are letters my grandfather and grandmother wrote to each other leading up to their wedding!"

"Oh, my." Scott said, looking down into the box. At the same moment, he heard Brie gasp.

"These are important. But I don't understand what that has to do with me."

"Don't you see?" Mother chided. "You are planning your wedding. I thought these would be perfect for you two."

Scott didn't know what to say. He just stared at the letters. This was something precious to entrust to him and Brie. It warmed Scott to think that his mother must think much of Brianne to share these. More than he'd thought.

"Thanks, Mom," Scott said slowly. He looked to Brie. The look on her face was unreadable. Was she awed as he was? Touched as he suspected? Something else? He hated that he was never very good at reading people.

"Yes, thank you." Brie's voice was timid.

Mother's smile spread over her whole face. "Go ahead, read one."

A timer beeped, and Mother looked toward the kitchen.

"Shoot, that's the roast. I just need to go check on that." She rose.

Brianne started to stand. "Do you need any help?"

Mother shook her head. "No, dear. You sit and relax."

Then Mother was through the door and out of the room.

Scott gingerly touched the stack. The script on the front was faded but fanciful. What a treasure. He focused on Brie. "Amazing, isn't it?"

She nodded, but her gaze remained fixed on the letters. "It really is." Her voice wavered.

He wrapped an arm around her and pulled her to himself for an embrace. "We can look at them later. For now, I'd rather sit here and enjoy you."

A shiver went through her. What was going on in that head of hers?

Pausing and closing his eyes, he prayed for guidance.

Brianne hated the quiet between her and Scott. Dinner with his parents had been awkward to say the least...even more so than usual. But how could she explain to him what was in her mind and heart without creating more challenges? So she remained quiet.

Scott sighed. He was likely very tired from the drive today. Combined with the strain of the mealtime. Though his mother had been eager for him to open the letters, he had excused himself from doing so, begging off that he was too tired to focus. And promised he would get to them soon.

"Are you okay?" Her voice was small even to her ears. But he had been so focused on her and how she was, it was time to direct her attention to him. After all, he had to have feelings, right?

He leaned toward her. "Yeah. I'm just tired of being in the car."

"I know." Guilt slammed into her. Visiting her parents and doing wedding stuff in Middle Tennessee was what pushed them into this three-hour drive almost every weekend. All because of her. But it was her wedding, right? It should be near her hometown. That's what was customary.

A gentle whisper in her thoughts reminded her that it was his wedding, too. Was she giving enough allowance for his wants and dreams?

Looking at her hands in her lap, she prayed that she would be more mindful. Listen better.

But that wasn't all. He seemed fatigued beyond the day.

She reached for his hand.

He weaved their fingers together and squeezed.

"I love you," she said, gazing at his profile.

He smiled at that. She only wished it wasn't such a tired smile. Still, it was genuine and it alleviated some of her guilt.

"I love you, too." But his gaze never left the road. That was to be expected. It was darker and he needed to be mindful of the conditions outside the car.

"Maybe some good sleep will help." Did she believe that? Not really.

He nodded. "Perhaps."

She could always count on two things from him: the truth and the benefit of the doubt. It was so good of him to give her the space she needed with her thoughts and support her along the way. Her prince. And she did love him so much.

"Something on your mind?" His question was delivered with a gentle tone, but there was worry underneath it. She sensed more than heard it.

"I...don't know."

The car fell into silence once more. Then he spoke. "Want to talk about it?"

"No." The word came out before she quite filled out her thought on a response.

He let out a long breath.

"What?" Her tone accused. Did she feel that way? Apparently so.

His eyebrows lifted. "Nothing."

"It doesn't sound like nothing." She grumbled. Why was her tone so biting? Where did this layer of animosity come from?

"Brie, let's not do this." His words were laced with weariness. Did he find her tiresome?

Dread filled her. What was he hiding? She pressed her voice into a quieter tone. "What exactly am I doing?"

She knew she was being a bit less mature than her age. Did this have to be so dramatic? Fighting within herself, her own emotions, she wondered if this was a reflection of things pushed down for too long. Were there things—feelings, thoughts—he wasn't voicing?

He squeezed her hand. "Brie..."

She slipped free of his grasp.

Switching on the right turn signal, Scott maneuvered the car into a nearby parking lot.

As he set the gear shift to park, she pressed out, "Why did you do that? I thought you were eager to drop me off and then get to your bed."

She didn't really know why she was striking out at him. Or how to stop the momentum that had started this.

He still gripped the steering wheel. "Just because I'm tired doesn't mean I want to get away from you."

"That's not what I'm saying." That was exactly what she was saying. But why? Did she need him to prove his love for her so much she would push this issue? That wasn't the grown up way to express oneself or to garner reassurance.

She dropped her head. She had two choices: continue down this path, or be brave enough to stop. Which meant apologizing and being vulnerable. "I'm sorry."

Nothing.

When she turned to look at him, his eyes, widened, were on her features. And there appeared to be a glint of moisture about them. A knife cut through her heart at the pain she caused him. Had that been her intention? It wasn't what she really wanted.

"What's going on? I wish you would tell me." He covered her hand, still on her lap, with his larger one, his thumb stroking her fingers.

She shrugged. The desire to hold it in was still strong. Could she share her jumbled thoughts? Let him talk her down? Part of her wanted that. But a bigger part feared he would dismiss her concerns. And she had them in spades.

"Talk to me, Brie." He leaned toward her, setting his other hand on her forearm.

She shook her head. "I don't know that I can."

His eyes glistened in the moonlight. So much emotion. And she was responsible for it.

She watched him as she tugged her hand free. "I want to. But I can't understand it for myself. There's so much."

"Didn't your counselor say that it's good to share? That the challenging thoughts only have power locked in your mind?"

She nodded. "But this is not like that." Her voice was neutral. Was she, too, worn with the conversation?

"Okay. Sorry."

She sensed his gaze even though she refused to look at him again. She couldn't. It was too disconcerting to see the lines of his features...the pain.

Then the pressure of his eyes on her alleviated.

She glanced at him.

He stared forward. And all was silent again.

What should she say? What could she do? She wanted desperately to reach out to him but didn't know quite how.

"I don't know what to do." His voice was soft. Turning, he met her gaze again. "I love you. So much it scares me."

"Scares you?"

"I've never felt anything like this before. I want to protect you. And I know that sometimes that means pushing you a little. I hate it, but I want you to be okay."

She fell a little more in love with him in that moment. Reaching out, she set a hand to the side of his face. "I know. And I will share. I just...need time."

He dropped his regard to the console between them then lifted his gaze to hers. "You mean the world to me."

She leaned across the center compartment as much as she could and pressed her lips to his. When the gentle kiss had served

16

to reconnect them and reaffirm her, she pulled back and set her forehead to his. "I know. You mean everything to me, too. We have to trust each other and trust God."

Was she saying this to him? Or more to herself? Either way, it was truth.

He placed a kiss on the tip of her nose, his warm breath caressing her features. "You're right."

"We should probably get going. My pillow is calling and I think yours is, too."

He smiled at that, slowly settled back into the driver's seat, and started the car.

One thing was certain: all the confusion and conflict within her was not going to permit her any sleep tonight.

# *letters*

*February 18, 2020*
*Trammel Apartments*
*Cordova, TN*

S cott dropped his keys on the kitchen's bar-height counter. He was tired. But he was also worried. Setting the shoebox from his mother on the end table in the living room, he fell onto the couch.

"That you?" The voice came from the second bedroom down the hall. Paul. Soon enough, his friend appeared at the door opening.

"Yeah. Didn't think you'd still be up."

Paul looked back into his room. "You know me. I was mixing a song."

"Oh? Anything I can listen to?"

Paul waved a hand at him. "Nothing like that. Just learning this mixer board. How was 'Clarks-vegas'?"

Scott rewarded his friend with a grin. "You need to quit calling it that."

"That doesn't answer my question."

Scott shrugged. "It was great hanging out with her parents. And the venue coordinator said they can work with our plan."

"But...?"

Scott rubbed a hand down his face. "I don't know."

Paul folded arms across his chest and leaned back against the frame. "You need to tell her what you're thinking, man."

Again, Scott shrugged. "Something's up with her. I sense it. But she doesn't want to talk about it...yet."

"So neither of you are communicating with the other?"

"I wouldn't say that."

"What would you say?"

Scott considered that and came up empty. "Same words, less ominous tone."

Paul chuckled. "I'm telling you...it's not going to be good for y'all to keep this stuff in."

"You sharing this from all your experience being engaged?"

Paul thrust his fist against his chest. "Ouch!"

Scott shook his head. "It's complicated. And there are a lot of emotions."

"I can only imagine. But, listen, the thing I always admired about your relationship is how open y'all have been over the last few years. Y'all spent enough time not sharing when it first started. I thought you two were past that."

Scott tried to take in the words and sift the truth. Honestly, it was all true. He and Brianne had fought hard for the closeness they shared. Was it worth it to risk all that just to spare her feelings? And maybe himself some discomfort?

"Get some sleep. You look exhausted." Paul went back into his room and called over his shoulder, "We can hash this out tomorrow."

"No, we won't," Scott yelled back.

A chuckle came from Paul's bedroom. And then silence. He'd

likely put his headphones back on and refocused on his work. Scott thanked God for such a friend. Not everyone would be willing to call him on his junk. Paul totally was. Maybe even enjoyed it a bit too much.

Either way, it was time for bed. He pulled himself up and trudged toward his room. What could be bothering Brianne? He hated seeing her like this. But his hands were tied. Once again, God was teaching him patience. Could he be done with the lesson? And that's one more reason God was having to teach him patience.

He stepped into his bedroom and let out a breath, hoping to expel all the tension in his body and turmoil in his heart. This engagement stuff was for the birds. He and Brie had never struggled quite like this when dating.

Their premarital counselor had warned that this time would be trying. *It's not all registries and sunshine*, the pastor had said. He was not kidding. But there was hope. Pastor Taylor had assured them that after the wedding all the stress eases and things are a bit easier.

Scott scanned his dresser with sleepy eyes. Brie was everywhere. A picture of the two of them sat on the edge of the dresser next to a couple of mementos gathered on dates. And, despite the tension of the evening, he smiled. She was it. And he was eager to really start their life together.

And the wedding was the big hump in between. He wanted it to be everything she had dreamed about. Hadn't he promised himself he would do what he could to make her happy?

Setting that in his mind, he moved to the chair in the corner and kicked his shoes off. He really should nab his pajamas, but he was just too tired.

He looked at the bed longingly and it was decided—sleeping in his clothes.

As he flopped onto the mattress, he sent up a prayer for his and Brie's marriage. And for the tension between them. He wanted to be the man God designed him to be. The man he needed to be for Brianne.

Then he gave himself over to sleep.

*February 20, 2020*
*Wyngate Apartments*
*Cordova, TN*

Brianne sipped her coffee. She was still tired. But she had given sleep her best shot. There was just too much weighing on her mind—the wedding, the virus, what the future might hold. And so, once again, she was thankful for coffee. Heavenly brew.

She settled on her couch, set her mug nearby on the end table, and pulled out her phone. Some days she hardly checked the thing. Then others, it was glued to her hand. Oh, well. Such is life.

Scrolling through her most recent emails left her a bit mortified. Her inbox had reached 7,000 unread messages. All time high. Somehow, she didn't feel like it was a win though. Maybe one day she'd go through and file or delete them. But for now, the inbox kept growing.

The text message notification dinged. It was Latasha.

How was the weekend?

What a big question. What to tell her? Her thumbs went into action almost before she formed her response in her head.

It was okay.

Okay? Uh oh. What's up?

Yep, Latasha knew her well...probably too well for comfort. But her friend loved her. That meant everything to Brianne.

> Nothing. It was fine. Not a lot to report.

> Come on. You are planning your WEDDING. It should be fantastic!

Brianne smiled.

> I'm sorry to disappoint.

The phone buzzed. Latasha's name flashed across the top of the screen.

Brianne didn't want to talk, though. Latasha wouldn't stop until she pulled the deeper things out. Was Brianne ready for that? She had brushed Scott's efforts to the side, perhaps she could do that with Latasha.

Swiping the bottom of the screen, she then hit the indicator for speaker phone. "Hey."

"Girl, you gotta spill. What's going on?"

Brianne sighed and sank farther into the couch cushions. "I'm honestly not really sure what I'm thinking."

"That's a smoke screen." Latasha always knew just how to prod.

"I'm just so...worried. Well, maybe that's not the right word. Maybe more 'concerned.'"

"What are you *concerned* about? Did you and Scott have a fight?"

"No, nothing so dramatic. I'm just so unsure about the wedding. He was pretty worn out by the time we got back to Memphis last night. What was I thinking planning a wedding so far away?"

"You were thinking about having it close to home."

"Yeah...but I didn't really think about what that would mean. All this back and forth."

"Burning up I-40 for sure."

Brianne laid her head back on the top of the couch.

"Listen, if you want to change the wedding plans a bit, that's fine."

"But the invitations have been printed already and a lot have been sent out." An unpleasant roiling in the pit of Brianne's stomach made her feel a little sick.

"It's not a big deal if you really want to change the venue."

Brianne frowned. It seemed like a big deal. Latasha was being sweet but a bit dismissive of the emotional cost of contacting all of her family and friends, some of whom might have made arrangements to fly into Nashville. Could they switch flights to Memphis? And if so, how would her parents feel about moving the event location? What about deposits put in at the bed and breakfast in Murfreesboro?

"You still there?" Latasha's voice had a hint of laughter to it. "Or have you spaced on me?"

"I'm here."

"I want to help, but I have this sinking suspicion that I've opened a can of worms."

"Oh, it was already open." Brianne groaned. "I want Scott to be happy. But I'm not sure what he would prefer."

"Well...this will probably be obvious, but you could ask him."

"Yeah. Then he'll want to talk."

"Oh goodness, a man who wants to know how you feel." This time Latasha outright laughed. "We should all be so lucky."

Brianne's smile grew despite herself. "Tom seems pretty concerned with how you feel."

"Not a chance. We're not deflecting onto me."

Man, strike out.

"Is there something else? This venue thing can't have you all tied up in this many knots."

Brianne played with the tasseled edge of her throw pillow. "I'm still nervous about this virus sweeping the nation."

"First of all, breathe. It seems pretty isolated. If everyone is responsible with keeping their butts home until they're better, it can be nipped. You're getting ahead of yourself."

Brianne nodded, but something held her back from settling herself to that argument. "What if it's not?"

"That's not a bad question. And what if it's not? God's got this."

That was certainly true. Then again...God never promised a life devoid of grief and suffering...Brianne knew that all too well. Just the opposite. Didn't the book of James read something like 'in this life you will have trials?'

"Earth to Brianne."

"Huh?"

"You did it again."

"Oh, sorry. I was just thinking."

"Okay. I'm coming over."

"I'm fine. No need to trouble yourself."

Latasha clicked her tongue. "Who said it was trouble? I'll be there in fifteen minutes."

Brianne wanted to naysay her, but experience told that it was useless. "Thanks, friend." Then she remembered. "Oh, and I think I'm low on coffee..."

"Um, there's a coffee shop on the way." The smile was evident in Latasha's voice.

"Oh. Okay. See you in a few."

The phone beeped and went silent.

How was Brianne supposed to hold it together? Her friend always knew just how to draw out Brianne's feelings and thoughts. And that scared Brianne more than anything else—her thoughts and feelings. She wasn't ready to delve into that place that could be so dark.

She sucked in a breath. *Give me strength, God. Don't let me fall apart.*

Then she downed the last of her coffee. She best get some regular clothes on. Then again...this was Latasha. What was the point of leaving the comfort of her jammies?

Settling back on the couch, Brianne reached for her phone again. Time to see what everyone had to say on Facebook.

*February 27, 2020*
*Trammel Apartments*
*Cordova, TN*

The week had flown by and yet dragged at the same time. Scott's time at the office went by slowly, but his after work hours had vanished too quickly. He and Brie had chatted on the phone and texted, but they had not had the chance to see each other.

Tonight, however, they would. Scott could hardly wait. After the week of complicated, he needed to hold her. As much for her as for him.

He walked into his apartment to find it dark and void of any life. Where was Paul? The guy typically didn't linger at his job. Too much eagerness with that sound board. Though he had yet to share any of his work with Scott. Oh well.

The couch and television called to him, but he wanted to wash the week off of him and get ready for his and Brianne's evening. So, he cut through the silent space toward his room.

His phone buzzed. Tugging it free of his pocket, he smiled. Brianne.

> Hey. You home?

A warm sensation filled him. The same feeling he got every time he was with her.

> Yeah. Can't wait to see you in a bit.

> :-) What is the plan?

His grin widened. She would be so excited.

> I thought we might go to Bahama Breeze. There's a key lime pie slice with your name on it.

Text bubbles played at the screen. And then didn't. Then again. Was she second guessing her response?

> We can go somewhere else if you'd like. I just want to see you.

More text bubbles. *Don't read too much into that,* he told himself. No use assuming anything.

> I'd rather just order pizza and watch a movie.

Pizza and a movie? That didn't sound like her. Not that she was high maintenance, but she never turned down key lime pie. Much less the one from Bahama Breeze.

Again, he wondered what filled her thoughts. She had seemed more distant of late. Maybe they'd have a chance to talk more openly in the privacy of her apartment.

> What time did you want me to come over?

> An hour? I'm eager to see you too. It's been a week.

He frowned. She'd had a hard week? It wasn't as if he hadn't seen the signs. But he didn't like to think of her struggling. He went to type out such but deleted it. They would have a chance to talk soon enough.

> K...what kind of pizza you want? Pepperoni or ground beef?

> Whatever you want.

He hated when they did this. They were both easy going enough that they could go back and forth for a while. So he sidestepped that minefield and made a suggestion. She liked Detroit style thick crust, or thin. It usually depended on many factors...information he didn't have. And he wasn't interested in a ton of back and forth.

> Thin crust pepperoni?

> Sounds great. See you in an hour.

Pocketing his phone, he then pulled out a fresh shirt and jeans. He had almost finished gathering the needed items when a key slid into the front door lock.

Scott set his things down and peered out of his room as Paul opened the door.

"Hey." Scott nodded at him.

"Hey." Paul gave him a mock salute. "It's Friday."

"Sure is. I'm about to hop in the shower."

"Oh yeah. Date night." Paul set his bag down and settled on the couch as he picked up the remote.

Paul always spent the first half hour or so back in the apartment doing some decompressing. For him, that usually meant a mindless sitcom.

Scott moved back down the hall toward the bathroom.

"Hey, Scott!" Paul called after him.

He turned. "What's up?"

"What's with this shoebox?" Paul pointed at the object still sitting on the end table. Had it been there all week? Scott had completely forgotten about it.

"Oh. That's something my mom gave me." Scott moved toward the heirloom.

"What is it?"

Scott gingerly lifted the lid and peered at the worn paper. "Some letters my great grandfather and great grandmother exchanged leading up to their wedding."

"And your mom thought you'd like to read them because you're planning a wedding." Paul shifted his focus back to the TV, scrolling channels.

"Yep." Scott felt the urge to investigate the box further. He flipped the box lid and secured it to the bottom of the box as he sat in the nearby chair.

Paul punched the volume up as he settled on his favorite show. "Weren't you gonna get a shower or something?"

"Yeah," Scott replied absent-mindedly as he looked through the letters. There were quite a few. Where would he even start? Were they in some sort of order?

His curiosity piqued, he untied the ribbon that made a cross hold on the stack. Sliding the first in the stack out, he examined the handwriting. It was a cursive flourish that had a blocklike quality to it. Not as smooth and flowy as the letter after it. Turning it over, he slid the back open and pulled the papers out.

The sound of the TV faded in Scott's mind as he homed in on the writing.

27th March 1918

Dear Rose,

Thank you for your permission to write you. I found you most fascinating. The moment I spotted you, it was my desire that we share more than a passing conversation.

I do hope you are well at Fort Riley. How do you find Kansas? I have heard that the sickness continues to spread. It is rather alarming...

## THREE

*a silent enemy*

*March 20, 1918*
*Camp Funston*
*Fort Riley, KS*

Dr. Theodore Hendry frowned and pulled his glasses off so he could rub the bridge of his nose. This did not look good. Not at all. He had come to Camp Funston on a mission. A research mission. There had been occurrences of a strange influenza. A rather curious flu. And the army needed fresh eyes on it. Those of a researcher at heart.

He examined the medical charts of the men and women who had died from the illness. And what he was finding baffled him. How could completely healthy men and women be brought down...and so quickly? It didn't make sense. These were individuals that should have been able to fight the flu. There was no logical reason they succumbed to it in such a way.

"Dr. Hendry." A man's voice interrupted his perusal of the medical documents.

Theodore looked up. Dr. Lance Donovan, his friend and guide

in this camp, stood in the now open doorway, a woman at his side.

Theodore stood out of deference to the lady. And a quick glance soon became a difficulty, for his gaze wanted to linger. Her blonde hair shone bright, even in these lights. And while her form was petite, her eyes held a fierceness to them. It drew him in all the more.

"Dr. Hendry?" Lance said again, before coughing.

He shook his head. "Sorry, Dr. Donovan. How can I help you?"

The man quirked the edges of his lips into a smirk that quickly disappeared.

Theodore wanted to punch the man. Or himself for his moment of thoughtlessness.

"This is one of our nurses, Rose Garrett." Lance held out a hand toward the woman who appeared to be sizing Theodore up.

Lance continued after a brief pause. Was he so amused by the sparks flying between his friend and this woman? "Nurse Garrett tended several of the patients lost to us in this last month."

Theodore leaned toward them and put out a hand. "Pleasure to meet you, Ms. Garrett."

She looked at his hand as if it were a curiosity then slid her smaller hand into his. "It is good of you to come, Dr. Hendry. We need answers."

"I assure you, finding those answers is my top priority." He tried to spot the presence of a ring on her left hand, but it was difficult the way she kept it tucked close to her body.

She offered him a small smile but still seemed rather put off. Was it him? The way he had stared? For he felt a great deal of electricity coursing through his veins—all the more at her touch. His body warmed and he was certain the heat would show in his face.

So he tugged free and pulled his hand back, tempted to put it in his pocket. My, wouldn't that seem odd?

Now she was studying him with a curiosity that brightened her green eyes even as it narrowed her gaze. Was she amused?

"Apologies, I forget my manners," he muttered. "May I talk to you for a few minutes?" He indicated a chair opposite his across the desk he had been lent to study over the records.

She gave a brief nod and stepped to the chair.

Theodore tore his gaze away long enough to give Lance, who was smiling like a Cheshire cat, a hard look. His friend simply shook his head and slipped from the room, leaving the door open enough to inhibit privacy, but not so much others would overhear easily.

Goodness, this was awkward. And likely to become more so when Lance got him alone. Theodore suppressed a groan.

"Mrs. Garrett," he started while taking his seat once more.

"It's Miss." Her correction was music to him. Unmarried. Perhaps even not engaged. Was she unconnected romantically?

"Miss." He offered what he hoped was a warm smile. Not a giddy one. Had he transported back in time? He was as awkward as a school boy.

She stared blankly at him.

Oh yes, the patients.

"Miss Garrett, I am so sorry you've had patients pass this way."

She nodded and her face became a mask of neutrality. Was it difficult for her to think about it? Would she be able to give him the answers he needed?

"I know this may be unpleasant..." An urge flared up in him to protect her from such difficult things, but that wasn't possible. He had to seek these answers. If they were going to uncover the root of this thing before it spread. "...but I need to know about them—the men and women under your care. Their symptoms, the progression of the illness..."

"Isn't all of that in the medical files?" Her tone held an under-current of accusation.

"It is. But I want to hear it in your words. You know as well as I do that charting can leave holes. Especially when it comes to details that may not seem significant at the time. I need to know everything."

She drew in a deep breath and pressed it out.

That desire to shield her again took hold, but he shoved it out of mind. He had a job to do. And he was asking her to do her job. This was not a moment to delve into something that may or may not be thickening the air between them.

"Just tell me what symptoms they had when brought to the hospital and anything you know about any symptomology before that." He kept his gaze on her...not that he would be able to tear it away. At least now he had a reason, and he hoped his gentle way would comfort her in some small measure.

She cleared her throat and straightened her shoulders, a courage settled over her demeanor. "By the time most were in my care, they had high fevers, dry coughs, widespread body aches, fatigue, and even chills."

Theodore nodded, all of these things had been recorded...and were expected with influenza. "Anything else? Even if it doesn't seem significant."

She thought for a moment. "Many did complain of sore throats. But with the season change, they all had runny noses as well. I assumed the two were related."

He frowned. Rose was correct, sore throats were common with congestion and drainage. But he wrote it down anyway. No sense in dismissing her observation. "What, if anything, did you find odd about the individuals who were infected?"

She watched him with twin emeralds. But there was some-thing more, a sheen of moisture, a sadness he couldn't quite account for, even considering how many people she had sat with at their passage into eternity. Had it affected her more deeply than he'd expect for someone who must have seen plenty of death in this senseless war?

Rose looked away.

He stood and moved around the desk. Again, he wanted to comfort her in some way. She was young. Too young to usher so many to their ends. But he folded his arms to keep them still as he sat against the desk's front.

She wiped at her eyes and met his gaze again. "They were all in their twenties and thirties."

He nodded. Yes, he had noticed this, too. So many falling victim to this illness did not fit the profile. These kinds of illnesses typically found the elderly and the youngest more susceptible. Not those who were in their prime of life.

"They shouldn't have died." Her voice broke at that, and she bit her lip while looking down at her hands in her lap.

"No," he said, his tone soft, "they shouldn't have. It doesn't make sense."

She peered up at him, not making an effort to hide the watering about her eyes.

He couldn't stop himself. Reaching out a hand, he gently touched her shoulder. Would she accept his touch? See it for what it was—a hope to ease her burden—or think him a cad?

She didn't pull away, but more tears came.

Tugging out his handkerchief, he offered it to her.

She paused but then lifted a shaking hand and took the proffered cloth.

"You must have cared a great deal for these poor souls," he said without a thought. His heart hammered in his chest, urging him to give her heart a soft place to land.

"Some were friends, and..." She stopped herself. Why?

"That must have made this even more difficult." He lifted the corners of his mouth, hoping to communicate his sympathy. "But there is hope. I want to get to the bottom of this. Find a treatment. A cure."

She nodded and pressed the handkerchief to her eyes. Why did that not ease her burden? But he knew.

"No one can bring back your friends, but I tell you, I will do what I can."

She shook her head. "I'm sorry for my emotion, Dr. Hendry."

"Don't be." His words were just above a whisper. Did they soothe her? "Losing a friend...or friends to this...the pain is understandable."

Her features became difficult to read. Almost a lack of emotion.

"What is it?" He couldn't stop himself from asking. "Did you think of something else?" Moving back around the desk, he grabbed for his notes and pen.

"Nothing helpful, I'm afraid."

"It just might be. You never know with these things," he said, quick to naysay her.

She met his gaze. "It's just that..."

"What?" If he were sitting, he'd certainly be perched on the edge of the chair.

"My last patient..." she said as fresh tears flowed. She did nothing to stop them, though.

"Yes?" He had his pen poised, ready to record the details.

"He wasn't just my friend; he was my fiancé."

Why had she said that? Rose dropped her head in her hands. What was wrong with her? Other, of course, than the slice of grief cutting to her core. Walter's death had rocked her. And dashed her faith in love. Perhaps even her faith in God. For what loving, merciful God would allow such suffering as they had seen between the great war and this sickness taking hold of one person after another?

A warm hand rubbed at her shoulder. Dr. Hendry. The man had such compassion. She truly felt understood.

"That must be difficult." His voice was tender and laced with concern.

She nodded, dabbing the handkerchief over her eyes before clearing the drainage in her nose in what must be a rather unlady-like burst. Wait. This was *his* handkerchief. And she had just blown the contents of her nose into it.

Peering up, she met his gaze. "I'm sorry."

"About what?" His brow furrowed. Did he not mind what she had just done?

She held out the soiled cloth square. "I...should have used mine."

He waved her off, a glimmer of a smile in his eyes. "No need to worry yourself. I have others." Urging the handkerchief back toward her he said, "You keep that."

She swallowed, unsure what to say or what to think. "Did you...have other questions for me?"

His gaze rested on hers for a few moments. "I do. But I don't think now is the time for me to delve into them."

Her face heated. He must think her a sentimental fool. Letting her emotions get the better of her. And for a nurse. She had seen much, experienced much that she'd rather not revisit. But there was a time and place for this grief. Not in the midst of an inter-view regarding the care of her patients.

"I can manage." She pressed her weaker emotions down and sat straighter.

The look he wore then was a curious one. Something between sympathy and disbelief. Did he not think her capable?

"It's not dire that we continue this at this moment. I think I have what I need in the records."

Her heart sank. Had he labeled her an uncontrolled female? She understood that many men...especially in the military, believed women to be of a weaker ilk and treated them likewise. That brought a flare of indignation.

"I told you, Dr. Hendry, I am quite able to answer your questions. I apologize for my outburst. It won't happen again."

He leaned back, effectively removing himself from the space around her. Why didn't he say anything? What was he thinking?

She blew out a breath, wishing it would loosen the tightened muscles about her heart.

"I thank you, Miss Garrett. But I think I'll spend some time in the clinical notes. But I may need to speak with you again." His voice had regained its firm baritone. There was little indication that he pitied her.

She nodded, grateful for his demeanor, and stood.

But as she made her way to the door, he called after her.

"I wondered, Miss Garrett..." He paused as if he considered his words. And he stepped closer to her. His arms remained folded over his chest. But instead of appearing defensive, it made him seem almost casual.

"Yes?" The word was too quiet. She cleared her throat of any lingering emotion. "Did you need something further?"

"I hoped I might be able to write you." Was he so brazen? He had been kind to her, but she had just told him her fiancé passed.

"I'm not sure I..." She searched for the right words, fighting against an ire rising in her stomach. He *had* been kind. There was no reason to think him so improper.

"If I have further questions about this illness, that is. Or if you think of other information you may not have thought to chart."

Of course. He was reaching out because of his research. Not for interest in her personally, but for this spreading flu. A part of her was almost disappointed at that. But that didn't make sense. She still mourned Walter, and she had no thought to risking her heart again.

She tilted her head. "That would be fine."

Something of a smile played at the corners of his mouth, but he suppressed it. Again, she was thankful for his sense of things. But she did find some delight in seeing it all the same.

Perhaps, with more men of Dr. Hendry's sort, there would be hope beyond her pain. And beyond this war.

# FOUR

## *fear becomes her*

*March 5, 2020*
*Wyngate Apartments*
*Cordova, TN*

Brianne looked at the clock once more and checked the text thread with Scott. Yep, he had said an hour. That was an hour and a half ago. Should she call him? Was there something keeping him? An accident maybe? Perhaps he hadn't called her about being late because he was incapable...unconscious even.

*That does it.*

She punched in Scott's number and prayed her mind was out of control.

"Hey," Scott's voice was the most wonderful sound.

She closed her eyes and breathed a prayer.

"What was that?"

"Nothing." She wiped at an errant tear. For certain, she was ridiculous.

"Sorry I'm late, sweetheart. I lost track of time." His voice sounded as apologetic as his words.

She felt torn between relief that he was okay and scoffing that she had taken second priority to something. "I'm just hungry."

"Well, I have pizza headed your way."

There was some clicking on Scott's end of the phone and a rustle of some sort.

"What's going on?" Brianne's shoulders tensed again.

"Just shifting the phone off speaker."

"Huh..." She pulled plates out of the cabinet. The hungry comment had not been an over exaggeration.

"Maybe I want to tell you sweet nothings and don't want anyone to overhear."

She smiled despite the rising trepidation. "I'll be glad when you're here..."

"Aww."

"...and I can finally eat!" She couldn't stop the laugh that burst forth.

"Well, my darling, your wait has come to an end."

The doorbell rang.

He was here? She rushed around the kitchen bar. "You are such a..." Flinging the door open, she was rewarded with the sight of her favorite person holding a box emblazoned with the name of her favorite pizza place.

"A what?" He flashed her a bright smile.

"A thoughtful man." She stepped into his one-armed embrace. But as soon as his arm came around her, the memories of her week rushed over her and a sadness came in its wake.

"Brie? You're trembling." He tugged her inside and kicked the door closed. The shuffle of the box told that he set it down on the entryway table and then his other arm wrapped around her, drawing her closer to himself.

She shook her head against his shoulder.

"It's okay. You can tell me." His voice weighed heavy with concern.

"I...I don't really kn-know what's wrong," she lied. It was just impossible to tell him.

He led her to the couch and urged her to sit.

She moved to lean into him again, but he halted her.

"Are you having doubts?" He looked so hurt, his eyes soft and his features tight. "Because, we don't have to—"

"No," she said, setting hands to his forearms. "It's not like that."

He eased visibly. "So, tell me."

She played with the fabric of his sleeve, examining it for something...she wasn't sure what.

"Brie, you've been tied up in knots for several days now... maybe longer. Please, talk to me."

She pushed out a long breath. Maybe it would help to talk about it. Besides, they were going to be married soon. It probably wasn't wise to keep so much of this pent up inside.

Her arms slackened, but he grabbed for her hands before she could pull them into her lap. His fingers stroked at her palms and wrists. It did soothe her.

"I am...so unsure what to think about this virus." Would he be frustrated to have this conversation again? With more information coming out, she was rapidly becoming more fearful.

Awareness lit his features. "I get that. It's a scary thing."

She let out some of the tension in her shoulders. "Yes. What is going to happen?"

"No one can know that. And..." He paused.

Why did he do that? Was he holding back? "What?"

He watched her for a moment before speaking. "I wish you weren't so plugged into what every news source is saying. There is so much information and misinformation out there. And I think you are trying to take it all in."

"Why wouldn't I? Don't we need to be in the know? We are planning a wedding...and the rest of our lives. Shouldn't we have some idea of what's happening with this virus sweeping the world?"

"That's not what I meant."

She knew that. This was a discussion they'd had before. Not that it ever ended with them in total agreement, but at least at some common understanding.

"I just think that so much of this is sensationalized. Scary headlines to incite viewers and make people feel like they have to watch...well, every news report." His eyes darkened a bit. It was true that he tended toward skepticism when it came to the media. No matter the source.

"I just...did you know there have been cases in Tennessee?"

He nodded. "Yes, I did."

If he didn't follow the news, how would he know that?

He chuckled a little. "Don't be surprised. I do keep tabs on what's happening. I just weigh what I hear and limit my sources."

Maybe he was right. Here he knew the same information she did without being bent out of shape about it.

"And besides," he said, setting a hand to the side of her face, "God is in control."

She nodded and looked down.

But he moved to capture her chin and tilt her face up. "He is, Brie. And we cannot thwart His plans or force anything to happen. Nor can we gain anything by stressing about it." His meaningful gaze softened again. He cared for her even if he didn't agree.

"That's true." She settled within herself. But a million 'what if...?' questions flooded her mind. How could she shut those off?

"Come here." He opened his arms to her again.

She only hesitated for a moment before snuggling against him. This was sure. This was security. And she wouldn't trade that for anything else.

"You ready to eat?" He pressed a kiss to the top of her head.

She nodded and started to stand.

He grabbed for her hand again, halting her. "Let me serve up the pizza while you find something fun to watch." Tilting his head toward the television, news still blaring, he offered a crooked smile.

"Of course." She nabbed the remote and switched it to one of the movie networks. She decided to put trust in Scott's words. They seemed reasonable.

But when he handed her a plate with pizza on it, she paused. On the one hand, her stomach ached for the nourishment. On the other, she wondered...what if someone in the kitchen at the pizza place was infected? What if Scott had crossed paths with someone that breathed COVID onto him?

While Scott took a big bite of the cheesy goodness, she couldn't help the turning in her stomach.

*March 31, 2020*
*Pyvot Technologies Offices*
*Memphis, TN*

Scott shut down his computer and rubbed at his eyes. He was doing the thing he always wanted to—writing code for a software company. But still, it was work sometimes. Thankfully, not often.

He longed for time to work on side projects at home. Though that would cut into his time with Brianne. And he was not willing to sacrifice any of that. Certainly not with her being in such a vulnerable state. She had come a long way in the last few years, dedicating herself to improving her mental health through medicine, counseling, and general awareness of what pulled her mood down.

He was proud of her. No two ways about it.

That didn't mean he had no worries. He did. She was everything to him, and he didn't like that there remained risk with her mood disorder.

"You headed home?" Jack's voice came from the cubicle's opening that served as his door.

"Yeah." Scott stretched his arms. "Finished coding that patch. So, I think it's a good place to call it a day."

"I'll say. It's past quitting time." Jack held up his watch.

Scott looked to his own timepiece. "Oh no." An hour past clock out time. How did he manage to lose track like this? He was deep in the code. And it just happened.

Thankfully, he wasn't meeting Brianne until much later. She had a late team meeting at work herself. Though she was likely getting out about this time. He hated the thought that his mindlessness would find her sitting somewhere waiting on him. Did she find that tiresome? Disappointing? She always seemed to find grace for him.

"Earth to Scott." Jack again.

"Yeah?" He turned his attention to Jack.

"You really are wiped out. Still got JavaScript on the brain?"

"Worse...Python."

"Ah." Jack shivered. "Not my favorite."

Scott let a crooked smile spread on his features. "I've got thoughts about incorporating a Spring library in Python."

"And here we are dragged into the world of software again." Jack shook his head.

Scott stood and slid his jacket on. It was the end of March in Memphis. There was a chill in the air yet. He grabbed his keys and wallet. "Let's go."

Jack turned and headed down the corridor of cubicles. A TV

was blaring in the corner of the lobby as the custodial staff worked in that space. Only, they weren't working. They were glued to the screen.

The governor was centered in the frame, giving a speech. What was it this time? A rehash of measures against the spread of COVID? Everything flashing on the screen made it look as though it was an important announcement.

Without a word between them, he and Jack paused to watch.

The governor announced that quarantines and social distancing had not been effective enough to slow the spread of the novel corona virus. So, at midnight, a shelter at home edict would be in place. Only essential work locations would remain open, such as grocery stores and gas stations. All other places of business would shut down, with telecommuting an option for many.

"Shelter at home?" Scott murmured.

"They've been talking about it for a couple of weeks," Jack said quietly. "It's already been in effect elsewhere. Guess it was bound to happen here."

Had Brianne heard about this? How was she feeling? Did she, likewise, see it coming? Or would she be overwhelmed by the pronouncement?

Scott had a vague thought that he should say something to the people around him, but his every thought was tuned to his fiancé. He had to get to her...now.

Rushing to his car, he pulled his phone out of his pocket and punched in Brianne's contact.

Nothing. Was something wrong? A wave of anxiety swept over him.

He looked at his phone. And he knew. It was likely the towers being overloaded.

Hitting his steering wheel in frustration, he pushed the start button and fired up his Honda. He had to calm himself as he wound out of the parking lot.

She was fine, she had to be.

*Lord...* he prayed silently, unwilling to give voice to his fears, but knowing they were best situated in God's hands. *Be with Brianne. Calm her fears. Help her lean on You. And help me get to her.*

As he came to the edge of the parking lot, he had a moment of crisis. Should he head toward her work? Or her apartment? Where was she most likely to be?

He glanced at the car's clock. Her apartment. Even if he got there first, he could wait.

Pulling onto the side street, he maneuvered his car around turns to get to Poplar. Only to find that it was jammed with cars. What had led to such uncharacteristic traffic?

The announcement.

Exactly where did everyone think they were going? It was past the normal day's closing hours for office-based businesses. Were people making a run on the grocery store? It wouldn't surprise him. All the news had to do was hint at snow or rain and there was mass demand for bread and milk. What, are they making milk sandwiches? That was typically his thought about that.

But right now, the traffic would keep him from Brianne. Which would be quicker—to try side roads or face the craziness that was Poplar?

He sat at the intersection for a moment longer and tried to dial Brianne again. His nerves were all knotted up in his stomach, almost sick with worry. Closing his eyes as the phone tried to connect, he prayed again. This time for his own worry and fears.

Opting for the harder route instead of wandering around side streets that may or may not prove efficient, he pulled into a space that appeared in the right most lane.

His heart thundered and his pulse raced, but he remained

mindful of his breathing...inhaling and exhaling as slowly as he could. There was only so much he could control. And traffic was not one of those things. But pray, he could. And he did. Every single painstaking inch of the thirty-minute drive to Cordova.

*March 31, 2020*
*The Vine Counseling Center*
*Memphis, TN*

*Shelter at home?* Brianne couldn't breathe. She couldn't move. This was monumental.

Without excusing herself, she backed toward the door of the conference room and slipped out. There would be questions from her coworkers, she was sure, but she couldn't stay in that room one moment longer.

One of the interns had called the meeting to a screeching halt when the news from the governor came through.

Nothing would ever be the same...ever.

Within moments, she was in her car and dousing her hands, arms—every surface she could—with sanitizer. Didn't even bother to grab everything from her desk. Who knew how long it would be until they returned? If ever.

She swallowed hard as she steered the car out onto Park Avenue. The real truth was that the spread of this virus would mean some of her coworkers, if not all, would contract COVID-19, and some would meet their end. It was just a reality. The mortality rate of this illness was high. Maybe higher than that of the flu. And that claimed thousands of lives every year, right?

Guilt slammed her at her abrupt retreat. Especially realizing that some of them she would never see again. How many? One or two? Or most? There was no way to know.

Though sadness spread through her awareness, it was not enough to drive her to return. She had to keep herself safe, after all.

The traffic was thick. People had just heard the same proclamation she had, no doubt. And they wanted to return home to some semblance of safety and security. But would that be safe? Would anything anywhere be safe again? Perhaps this virus would claim *her* life.

She shook her head; that wasn't necessarily going to happen. There was reason to believe she could control her environment enough to stay safe. Sanitize every square inch of her apartment, tuck herself securely within, and wipe down everything that came in through her door with alcohol. She could do it.

Her clothes should probably be recleaned as well. She'd start on that this evening. While she rid every part of her apartment from potential germs.

Sucking in a breath, she settled into the seat more. It was possible, and it was the only responsible thing to do.

It wasn't long before she pulled into the complex's parking lot. Someone was in her assigned space—not an odd occurrence, but more problematic today. She didn't want to have to repark later. Especially since her car would be parked for some time.

Still, the urge to shut herself into her own space drove her to take a guest spot. She would have to deal with the parking issue later.

Brianne grabbed her bottle of sanitizer and her tote bag, then stepped from the car and kicked the door closed. Oh dear, her shoes likely had all manner of germs on them. They would have to be cleaned as well.

Dripping sanitizer onto her hands as she walked to her first floor apartment in the back of the building, she rubbed antibacterial slicked hands over her tote bag strap to clean it. Then she smeared even more on the apartment's door knob. She inserted her key, careful not to touch any part of the door beyond the knob. It was tricky, but she managed.

Then she leaned back against the door from the inside. There was so much work ahead of her. And she'd best get to it.

Almost forty-five minutes later, she had scrubbed down the kitchen and had a load of laundry going. It would take probably the rest of the week to clean all of her clothes. Still, she would do it. Turning her attention to the small living room, she dragged out her baking soda, vinegar, bleach, and scrub brushes. Maybe she should make a solution and spray down everything. Scrubbing the carpet and sofa cushions didn't seem plausible.

A loud knock sounded on her door. She nearly lost her hold on her cleaning products. Who would disturb her at a time like this?

She moved closer to the door, but it had not been properly cleaned, so she was careful to stay a couple of inches away. "Who is it?"

"Oh, Brianne, thank the Lord you're okay."

Scott? What was she to do? He was not one to routinely sanitize. She had let it go until now, but this virus was vicious and out of hand.

She heard Scott press against the door. Then he spoke up, frustration evident in his voice. "The door is locked."

Fear crept through her. She couldn't let him in. Not until she had cleaned everything. Not until she was sure he was safe to touch. He might have the virus on him. Then he would track it into her apartment, into the only safe place she had. She called out, "Did you see the governor's announcement?"

"Yes. I came here immediately. I needed to see you. To make sure you're okay."

"I'm fine," she lied. Even she heard the waver in her voice.

"Then why won't you open the door?" His tone belied his exasperation.

"Scott, I...I can't." That was the truth. She couldn't let him walk in here. Not after...

"Brie, I'm worried about you. Just open the door. It's fine." He had lowered his voice to a reasonable level. Because he was concerned? Or because he didn't want to make a scene outside of her apartment?

Either way, she was unable to move closer to the door. Paralyzed. What froze her movements? A desire to stay safe? Or the belief that he was not clean?

"Please understand," she said, trying to keep her voice calm. "I...don't know what to do."

"Then let me in and we'll figure it out together." His words were firm, with a hint of pleading.

How could she shut him out? With all they were to each other...with their commitment to a life together. She knew...she *knew* she was being extreme. But she couldn't help it. "I need you to go."

"What?" The word dripped with astonishment.

"Please...I just need some time to wrap my mind around all of this."

Silence.

"Scott?" Part of her wanted him to have walked away...even if it was in a huff. But that wasn't like him.

"I'm asking you...don't shut everything and everyone out."

That wasn't what she was doing. But it was. She couldn't imagine that she would let anyone in.

"Even if you can't trust me, go to your folks' house. Or to Latasha's house. Or have someone come here. I just don't think it's a good idea for you to weather this alone."

She jerked back. "Not trust you? This has nothing to do with whether or not I trust you."

"No?" he challenged. The nuances of his words were getting harder and harder to discern through the door. Or perhaps through the veil of her thickening emotions.

"I do trust you. I just...the governor gave an order, and I intend to do what I can to follow it, to stop the spread of this horrid coronavirus."

"Even so, that starts at midnight."

That was true. How could she make him understand?

A thud on her door made her think he had pressed his forehead there. She could picture him leaning against it, reaching for her.

"Please, Brie. Let me in. Or at least open the door so I can see you're all right."

She tightened her lips in resolve. She was outright refusing him—the man she claimed to love, the man she planned to marry. How could she be this way?

But any thought to the contrary—letting him in, interacting with anyone—was too much to bear.

"I need you to understand." Her voice was a whimper. "I just need a couple of days."

She heard shuffling as if his hand moved over the door.

"Okay. But know that I love you. And I'm here."

Brianne bit at her lip to keep from outright crying.

"Listen, the cell towers seem to be overloaded, but text me. It may take a bit to get through, but I have no doubt it will get to me. Will you do that?"

She nodded then realized he couldn't see her. "Yes. I promise."

Holding her breath to hear better, she thought there was an exhale on the other side of the door but no movement. Was he still there?

She waited a couple of minutes, and then another scraping sound filtered through. Had he pushed himself off the surface and moved back? As she strained her ears, she thought she could make out slow footfalls on the concrete beyond the door. And so he was gone.

Sinking to her knees, she wailed and did nothing to stop the tears. Maybe they would cleanse her soul.

# FIVE

# loss and hardship

2 April 1918

Dr. Hendry,

Everything about the state of the world is horrid—the war to end all wars, this plague upon our post...all of it. No doubt you have heard that since you left, the number of cases within Camp Funston and the surrounding area has quadrupled. There seems little we can do to help. Some doctors here favor treating with aspirin, but I don't see much difference in the patients that take it. Many recover, but a few...they do not. Have you discovered any reason why? Why do some pull through and others do not? Especially those of young age and good health...

Rose paused mid-sentence, pen still resting on the paper. Why was she doing this? Yes, he had asked for regular communication about the illness in the camp. And yes, he had written her in that vein. But it still didn't make sense why he sought *her* out. Why not get his information from one of the physicians? Unless...there was more to his request to exchange letters. Did he seek to establish some connection with her?

She looked back over what she had written and wondered. Was this the kind of letter she would write to an overseer? Or to a friend? It felt more friendly. Why would that be? She had only briefly met the man. He had been kind, considerate, and compassionate in the midst of her break down. Something that still brought heat to her face.

But that didn't mean she should push aside her grief and memories of Walter so easily.

Guilt washed over her. Was that what she did?

Pushing the letter to the side, she set her pen down and let herself feel the full force of it.

It was not pleasant.

Did she seek to escape the inevitable pain by exchanging letters with this man? Was that why she imagined more between her and Dr. Hendry than there was? Or that he sought more than he maybe should?

Enough accusations. There was little basis for such assumptions. He asked for her to keep him abreast of all that happened pursuant to his research.

She picked up her pen again. Perhaps she only needed to be reminded of her purpose in writing.

*As the sickness spreads, I am concerned about the civilians. With so many medical staff away on the front lines, are there enough of us stateside to see to the growing number of cases?*

"Nurse Garrett," a woman breathed out as she paused in the doorway.

Senses immediately on alert, Rose turned to her. "What is it?"

"You are needed...Dr. Donovan...requested you come." Her rapid inhales and exhales as her breathing evened made her more difficult to understand.

Rose was on her feet in an instant. "Where is he?"

"Sick ward. Nurse Collins."

Rose's eyes widened as she sped out the door. Aubrey had been doing so well. Recovering nicely. What was amiss? More tender feelings for her friend threatened Rose's resolve, but she pushed them down. This was not the time for that. She must cover that vulnerability and perform her duties. Whatever that entailed in this instance.

An errant tear fell and Rose brushed it away, determined there would not be more.

In a matter of seconds, she approached Aubrey's cot to see Dr. Donovan leaning over her. Did he examine her or speak with her? It was difficult to discern.

Dare she speak up and interrupt him? That gave Rose reason to pause, but she inched closer to his position.

At length, he did rise.

"Doctor, you asked for me?" Her words were firm, but her tone was weaker than it should be.

He turned green eyes on her. They were dulled. By the many patients lost? Or by fatigue from caring for so many without respite?

"Doctor?" Some of her fear seeped into her voice. She cleared her throat. "How is she?"

He shook his head. "Nothing I am doing is helping her." He looked off, scanning the ward full of sickbeds. "Or any of them."

Rose pressed lips together. Partly to shut in her emotion. Partly to keep from consoling him. It would not be welcomed. Instead, she nodded.

"I..." He rubbed the back of his neck. "I thought we might need to do more here, but I think it would be best to call for the chaplain."

Rose's heart sank. Though she had not expected any different. Still, she pushed out. "Yes, doctor."

He dropped his gaze and put a hand to her shoulder in a companionable way. Indeed, they had seen much together, fought against this thief of a sickness together, and lost many patients... together. "Let us pray that Dr. Hendry might find an answer. And fast."

She couldn't venture an answer to that. But in her core, she knew he was right. That would be the only way out of this nightmare—answers.

As Dr. Donovan walked away, Rose set her focus on Aubrey who had fought valiantly as well, working alongside the rest of the staff here. A capable nurse. And now she was succumbing so young...too young.

Rose scooted closer to her friend, settling on the side of the cot. She bit at her lip to keep the tears at bay as she reached for Aubrey's hand. The woman lay still, and her arm did not burn with fever, rather it had cooled.

"Aubrey," Rose whispered. She knew she needed to get the chaplain so that he might be with Aubrey during her final moments, but Rose couldn't move. Didn't want to leave her friend and fellow nurse for the chance the woman would slip away alone.

Her friend mumbled something, but it was indistinguishable.

Rose did not fight the tears that streaked down her face as she leaned closer to Aubrey's ear and prayed for her.

It seemed the most logical...and even the right thing to do. There was a fear in the back of Rose's mind that she should not be so close to someone infected with this unseen killer. But she pushed that thought away. She would not deny who she was and withhold comfort to one who had labored well and for her efforts, paid with her life.

As Rose concluded her prayer, she whispered, "Rest now, my sweet friend. All is well."

The lines on Aubrey's face smoothed.

Rose watched as the rise and fall of Aubrey's chest became ragged and weak.

A hand on Rose's shoulder startled her, causing her to jerk around.

There was the chaplain, a sympathetic look upon his face. "Allow me."

Rose nodded but did not release her friend's hand.

The chaplain moved to the other side of Aubrey's cot and spoke Scripture over her.

It was not the first time she and this man ushered someone out of this world. And she hated that it would, for certain, be far from the last.

Theodore finished Rose's letter and set it down. It had started more businesslike, perhaps a bit forlorn. But it ended with her sadness seeping into the words. What had changed the tone of her writing? But he knew. She must have lost another patient.

He frowned. The tug of her sorrow penetrating his heart more than it should. Had he opened himself to feel such for her? Not so soon. Certainly not after such a brief interaction.

Yet there it was. Undeniable.

His gaze caught the timepiece on his desk. The meeting with his commanding officer was in five minutes.

Drawing in a deep breath, he both relished and regretted reading her letter right away. For now he had to push aside his concern to prepare for what he needed to say. And defend.

Grabbing the folders to his right, he stood then spotted her fine script atop the spread out papers.

He lifted it, folded it, slipped it back into its envelope, and placed it securely in a desk drawer. No need to risk someone discovering it. There was something...personal...about the way she had written. And he would protect that.

Letting out a sigh that he wished could press out the strain between his shoulder blades, he straightened and, clutching the folders, left his desk.

Moments later, he was at the office door. For what he intended to impart would not be received well. Still, he marshaled his courage and knocked.

"Come in," the Staff Sergeant called. His deep voice nearly vibrated the space around him.

Pressing into the door, Theodore swung it wide and entered.

"Ah, Dr. Hendry, glad you could come on such short notice." The man seemed quite pleased to see Theodore, but that didn't make sense. Did Staff Sergeant Higgins not suspect how difficult this exchange would be?

Theodore nodded and offered the man a small smile as he closed the door and took the seat opposite his commanding officer.

"How was your time at Fort Riley?" The man jumped right in.

It was refreshing and one of the things Theodore respected most in this man.

An image of Rose flashed in Theodore's mind. How was she truly? He even started composing his response but pushed that to the side. He was here to speak with Higgins about what he had learned.

"The situation is dire. And becoming more so." If Higgins didn't see the need to mince words, neither would Theodore.

"Oh?" Higgins eyebrows lifted. He couldn't really be surprised to hear this.

"This flu has some...irregular qualities to it." That was putting it lightly.

"How so?" Higgins leaned forward.

"It spreads extremely fast...probably worsened by the cramped conditions at the camp. And, while some recover once contracting it, others do not."

"You can't mean to tell me this is odd." Now the man leaned back and steepled his fingers. "Soldiers often die just as civilians do with seasonal illnesses."

"That's true, but most have some sort of pre-existing condition." Theodore did what he could to keep his tone in check, but he also wanted to communicate just how dire the situation was. "With this sickness, it strikes at those in the prime of life. An age group that is typically all but immune to fatalities from the flu. And these are healthy men and women. It makes no sense."

"Hmmm..."

"And," Theodore pressed in before Higgins could speak further, "the numbers have quadrupled since my time there. It has even gone beyond the base to infect civilians."

"Is that so strange?" Higgins was the picture of skepticism. "The flu sweeps the population every now and again—civilians and soldiers alike."

"This is no typical flu." Theodore's words were curt.

"It may be a stronger flu, but certainly no cause for such concern."

"It is my medical opinion that it is, in fact, cause for much concern. In fact, I recommend a full quarantine of the area. And we have to let the local population know about the spread."

Then Higgins's eyes darkened slightly. "Can you imagine what such information would do? There would be mass hysteria and fear. Surely, there is no cause for that."

Theodore recoiled. He had expected push back. But the staff sergeant's words held a finality to them. As if he had decided already what would happen.

"Besides," Higgins stood and moved around the desk. "We need to keep everyone's spirits up. There is reason to not distract them from their support of the war effort. We are in too deep."

"I understand. But this is no small thing. It could become much bigger...of epidemic proportions. We should not bury it."

Higgins sighed. "That is exactly what we will do."

"Pardon?" Theodore scoffed. Higgins couldn't mean that.

"The decision has been made. It comes from the top. We will do what we can to contain it, but we will also make every effort to preserve the nation's goodwill."

Theodore was certain his features had become stone, but his insides were twisted in knots. How could this be the answer? Yes, he was looking at only one piece of the puzzle, but it had the potential to wipe out hundreds. They had to stop it.

"I implore you, sir, reconsider. Write your superiors. Express my concerns."

Higgins offered him a sympathetic look, but there was not much behind it. "I can see that you are distressed. But I am asking you to do your job and let me do mine."

Theodore nodded, defeated. There was no leeway in the military for him to disobey direct orders. But he would do what he could to help those at Fort Riley. But how could he tell Rose he had failed her?

# separation

*April 1, 2020*
*Trammel Apartments*
*Cordova, TN*

S cott set his great-grandfather's letter to the side. He couldn't stomach any more at the moment, too distracted with his own plight, with the current measures pressed on him and the rest of the population. As well, his unplanned separation from Brianne.

His heart ached for her. What must she be feeling? Thinking? And so extremely that she would shut him out? If only he could enfold her in his arms and kiss away the fears. But he knew that he couldn't. And even if he could, it wasn't truly his place. He had no control over the future of this pandemic. Only God did.

Closing his eyes, he lifted yet another prayer for her. Seeking that God would gather her to Himself and protect her from the dark places she had been to and from the lies of the enemy.

As he finished, he felt a small measure of peace, but his stomach still twisted as he thought of her. She was shut up in her apartment. Alone. Would she reach out to Latasha? Would she let him reach out to her?

Perhaps now was the right time to try.

He picked up his phone and hit the call button.

Nothing.

He grimaced. Her inability to answer his call physically hurt and worried him.

Praying again, he turned even that over to God.

Maybe she would respond to a text?

His phone pinged.

> Hey…I was running the vacuum and didn't hear the phone.

Was that the truth? Or was she covering up for her inability to face him?

He typed out a response:

> Should I call now?

Text bubbles dotted his screen.

> No. I need to keep at it.

What was he doing here? He needed to be upfront with her, but he didn't want to intimidate. Yet he did want to speak truth as she would hear it.

> Can you just text for a minute?

> Okay.

He could almost hear the resigned sigh through the screen. But he would take any opportunity with both hands.

> How are you?

Text bubbles.
He waited.

> I'm good.

He didn't believe that.

> Do you need anything?

> I don't think so. But I will need groceries eventually.

What had it cost her to admit that she had a need?

> I could bring some to your door.

He waited. Not even bubbles. Then the ping.

> I would appreciate that.

The tension left his body on an exhale. That was something.

> You just let me know what you need and when.

> Okay.

> I know you're busy right now, but would you be able to FaceTime later?

He held his breath as he waited for the next ping.

> I guess that would work. I may be a sight.

He smiled.

> A sight for sore eyes for certain.

She sent a smiling emoji.

Sucking in a breath, he knew he needed to share his heart and sent.

> I miss you.

> I miss you, too.

That warmed his heart. When she had faced down her depression before, she had pushed him away. Hopefully, this was a sign that wouldn't be repeated now.

Again, he found himself wanting to respect the distance she seemed to be creating but needing to express himself. So, he sucked in a breath and pressed in.

> I wish I could be with you.

There was a long pause in the messages. Would she see it for what it was? Or feel cornered?

His phone screen went dark from inactivity. He closed his eyes, praying for understanding.

Then another ping.

> I wish that, too. But I just can't.

Lifting his phone, his thumbs flew across the small keypad.

> I know. I am trying to understand. I just want you to know that I'm here. And I love you.

He let out a long breath.

The next ping came much quicker.

I love you more.

He smiled. There was, then, hope. Those words were a balm to his wounded heart. He clutched the phone tightly in his grip. As if he could hold her hand and keep her from sinking deeper. In truth, he would do whatever he could to stop that slide into the darkness.

I need to get back to the cleaning.

It was likely a ploy, but Scott didn't mind. The words they had exchanged were probably difficult for her vulnerable state. But she had pushed into the conversation anyway.

And that was a win.

*April 10, 2020*
*Wyngate Apartments*
*Cordova, TN*

Brianne wished she could burrow into her couch. She sat cross-legged on the edge of the cushions, leaning over the armrest to stare at her phone. It was time. And she knew it.

The truth was that it wasn't good for her to isolate and shut everyone out. She had hoped Scott would understand, and their text conversations over the last couple of days gave her room to think it was possible.

Now, she had to fulfill a promise she made to him. She had to reach out to Latasha.

In truth, she wondered how her friend fared. But she knew that Latasha would prefer a phone call to a text. Yet was Brianne able to give that? She stared at Latasha's contact information and wished for the courage to call.

One of those court television shows was on in the background. Brianne only gave it part of her attention. Nothing important. Nothing pressing on her. Just...well, mostly nonsense.

But the words 'Breaking News' flashed on the screen. She reached for the remote and turned up the volume. Latasha could wait.

The picture cut to a podium with the American flag and Tennessee flag in the background. Soon enough the governor stepped in the room and took his place at the podium. Everyone in visual range of the camera was well spaced at the venue.

She focused in as the man flipped through his papers and shared the latest information on the state of things in Tennessee. Numbers that meant little to her and measures they wanted everyone to take were at the forefront of the discussion. It was old news by now, but she found some level of comfort in the reminders.

Masking outdoors. Check.

Limit activity. Check.

Make only essential trips outside for groceries and gas. Check —well, she hadn't been out of her home since the lockdown was set in place.

Social distance when you must go out. Check.

Stay calm. Che— well, she was doing that as much as humanly possible. So, check.

The head of the health department for the state stepped into the governor's place and droned on about new information, which was not new. Medical staff were working around the clock and researchers were doing what they could to work on a cure and a vaccination.

Though it was old news, she knew it was true. The whole of the populace had staked their hope in these measures and the eventual treatments that would potentially become available.

The speech droned on, but she turned the volume down and looked to her phone again. Latasha no doubt waited for her call. They had texted a little, but her friend deserved something more from her. After all they'd been through together, Latasha had earned the right to speak into Brianne's life. That was intimidating. Because it was certain there was a better, wiser way for Brianne to handle this, but this was the only path she could take.

Swallowing her trepidation, she punched the call button.

She gritted her teeth while the phone rang, having to hold herself back from hanging up with each ring.

"Hello?" Her friend's voice sounded rushed. Or breathless. Could she have developed COVID?

"You okay?" Brianne gripped the phone even as she pressed it to her ear.

"Yeah. I was across the room from my phone and I stumbled a little." Latasha laughed at her apparent clumsiness. "What are you going to do with such an accident prone friend?"

Brianne blew out a slight laugh despite the anxiety that had taken hold. Latasha was fine. Everything was fine. She cleared her throat. "I just wanted to check in on you."

"Sure. How are you?" Latasha's voice betrayed her concern no matter how she might choose her words.

"I'm good." That was the best answer she could give.

"Really?" There was that probing that Brianne had been afraid of.

"Yeah. Why wouldn't I be?" Immediately, Brianne regretted her defensiveness.

"I'm just worried about you there in that apartment all alone."

Latasha was only being honest. Shouldn't Brianne give her the same?

"Yeah, I know." Brianne took in a couple slow breaths. "I am fine. I have what I need here." *And I'm not putting myself at additional risk with other people to traipse in and out of here.*

"What do you do all day?" Latasha seemed genuinely curious.

Brianne played with the fabric of her night shirt. She hadn't showered in days. But she couldn't say that. Though, really, was there a point to keeping up her appearance? "I am getting some things done for the office online. They are trying to switch to a virtual model so that clients can still receive counseling."

"I think that's a great idea. So many will need that regular check in." No judgment, no pointing fingers...Latasha just spoke plainly. And she wasn't wrong.

Brianne had spent some time the last couple of days reaching out to clients to cancel appointments and speak with them about the virtual option. Many were glad. More were uncertain.

"You got all quiet." Latasha spoke into the silence.

"Sorry. Lost in thought. What are you doing to keep busy?"

"What am I not doing? I got my paint stuff out and set up my canvas stand by a window. I'm in heaven having so much time to devote to it."

Brianne smiled. That must be nice. Maybe she should do some doodling and sketching of her limited view out the back. It was a grassy area, though not huge. She would have to go out on the tiny patio to see farther.

That made her uneasy.

"I'm glad to hear it." She thought about what else she might say. But Latasha beat her to it. "Are you lonely?"

How to answer that?

"You could come stay in my parents' guest room. Or go to your own folks' house."

"But...we're supposed to shelter at home."

"You know what that means. They want everyone to stay put. Not gallivanting around town. Lord knows if those earlier cases had stayed put like they were supposed to, we might not be in this mess."

Brianne had reason to doubt that. This virus seemed to infiltrate and spread regardless of what they did or did not do.

"We might have even nipped this thing in the bud."

Brianne allowed a slight chuckle. Though she remembered the news talking about college-aged individuals throwing COVID parties. It made her shudder to think about it.

"Thanks, but I think I'll stay here. I do appreciate the offer, friend."

"Well, I won't pretend I understand, and I won't pretend I think it's best. It can't be healthy to hunker down with no one to interact with."

"Thank goodness for technology. I text with Scott several times a day. And I'm on the phone with you right now."

"Ha, ha." She sputtered. "Wait...you *text* with Scott? You aren't FaceTiming or video conferencing to see each other?"

What could Brianne say about that? Truly, it wasn't any of Latasha's business. But she couldn't say that. "I...am planning to FaceTime him today." She grimaced at her lie. Her unkempt appearance spoke to that. Perhaps, though, she might get a shower and make good on her statement.

"Okay...I just worry about you."

"I know. But I'm doing what I can to stay safe and well. I definitely plan to keep my sessions going with my counselor."

"There's the benefit to working in the administration of the center. You probably get first dibs on time."

Brianne was ready for this conversation to be over, but she was reluctant to do so just the same. "Nothing like that. I'm willing to take any time available after everyone else secures their appointment."

"Just remember that your mental health is important too."

Why did Latasha take on that mothering tone? Speaking of which, Brianne had missed yet another call from her mother. She tired of her mother's insistence that she make the trip home. Were all of Brianne's people crazy? She had every intention to stay put. "I promise. I'd best get back to work. I have some emails to send out. I haven't been able to reach a few of the clients by phone."

"Okay. But call me tomorrow."

"I will." Brianne hoped she would have the courage to do so. This had drained her more than she'd thought it would. "Till tomorrow."

"Tomorrow," Latasha repeated with emphasis.

Brianne pulled her phone away from her ear and clicked the end call button. Then she leaned back against the couch and just sank further into it. Had this range of emotions and her tendency to fight the advice of her friends become her normal? How much longer could she manage it?

She decided to let that be tomorrow's problem. Grabbing for her throw blanket, she lay across the couch, and turned up the television. Another judge show was coming on. What manner of ridiculous would today's episode have?

*April 15, 2020*
*Wyngate Apartments*
*Cordova, TN*

Scott looked over at the couple of bags of groceries secured in his passenger seat. He would be certain they were not crushed before they got to Brianne.

He had been thrilled she reached out to him. And a part of him dared believe she might open the door and he might see her. Not that he would push. Or even ask to come in should she open the door. Just to see her...and ensure she was well...was enough for him.

A thrill of anticipation shot through him. And he tamped it down. There was no reason to think she would. But there was the slightest sliver of hope.

He pulled into her apartment complex and wound around to her building. Grabbing the bread and eggs from his passenger seat, he then circled around to the trunk to get more bags.

His mother had insisted he do curbside pickup at the grocery store. Not that he felt there was a need to do so, but she was avid about it, and it was a small thing to ease her mind.

Then they had no contact curbside in addition. The gentleman had worn a mask and he was asked to mask as well. What was with that? He'd heard plenty about the masking. How it absolutely must be and how it would protect everyone from the virus. There were equally as many reports saying just the opposite.

Oh well. It didn't hurt him to comply if it made others feel better. After all, Jesus had talked about consideration and love for neighbors. If wearing a mask appeased others and made them feel safer, then he would do it. Not because he believed it would keep him safe.

He toted the bags down the silent corridor to Brianne's apartment, his anticipation growing with each step. Upon setting the groceries on the ground, he knocked on the door. And waited, praying with every breath that she might find a reason to open the door to him.

"Who is it?" she called through the door. She had to at least suspect that it was him. But the tension in her voice and wavering of her tone told that she was anxious at best.

"It's Scott, Brie. I've brought your groceries." He waited, his heart thudding in his chest.

"Thank you. Could you leave them there outside the door?"

The words dropped like an anchor that weighed in his stomach as he dropped his head.

"Scott?" Her words still trembled. As if she were fearful he might push her to let him in. Or that she worried he might become upset.

"I'm here." He set a hand against the door's surface, wishing he could touch the woman beyond it but knowing that he loved her too much to pressure her.

"I'm sorry. But I need you to just leave them there and go." It was said with finality.

"Of course, sweetheart. Please, let me know if you need anything else." He forced his hand away from the door and turned.

There was scuffling on her side of the door that drew his attention back around. Did she lean on it? Maybe even look through the peephole to see him? He could imagine that was so. Imagine that she missed him half as much as he missed her.

He took some breaths and realized…if she was looking out her peephole, it was likely to ensure he had walked away so she could gather her groceries. Again, his heart weighed heavy in his chest.

So great was the swell of emotion that he turned without anything further and walked slowly back to his car.

Pressing the ignition, he waited. Could he catch sight of her collecting her groceries?

Some moments later, the door opened. She stepped out, in a mask, glanced to the right and left. If he had to guess, he would say those were her pajamas. And her hair hung loose but did not appear to have been tended. What was that? Perhaps she had little reason to care for how she presented during this lockdown. He had gone longer between showers. Yet, this had been one of the signs of her descent into that dark place before. The memories of that tore at him.

With hands encased in yellow cleaning gloves, Brianne pulled her groceries out of the bags and into the apartment. Then she swept up the empty plastic grocery sacks into a trash bag.

And she was gone. Back inside. To the cell she had created for herself.

Why must he see it that way? She may feel that it had become a safe haven. But he wasn't convinced of that either.

Before he could stop himself, he swiped his phone open and punched the button for FaceTime. Then he selected her number.

It rang.

Would she answer?

It continued to ring...and just as he was preparing to give up, the screen came to life. And there she was, looking at him.

Though he couldn't touch her, he breathed out a long, ragged breath as emotion overwhelmed him.

She had pulled her hair back since he'd spied her at the door. Because she had gotten heated or because she didn't want him to see her hair wild? And she didn't have on makeup...not that she ever needed it.

"Brie..." Her name was all he could manage. He fought back a thickness in his throat.

"Hey." The word was brief, but it meant everything to him as she actually smiled.

"I...I miss you so much," he confessed.

"I know. I miss you, too." Her eyes glistened and she swiped at them.

"I just...wish we didn't have to be apart."

She frowned and opened her mouth.

He cut her off. "But...I understand that it has to be this way now."

She closed her mouth and chewed at her bottom lip.

"I'll take what I can get for the time being." He offered a smile he only partly felt. If only he could reach out and caress her face. But if this is what she was willing to give him, he would accept it with gratitude.

"Thank you. I just...don't know."

"Don't know what?"

"How to feel. What to think. It's all so crazy."

"Yeah, I know." He leaned back against his seat, relaxing into their conversation.

"There is so much coming at us, you know?"

He nodded. "I do. Information overload, if you ask me."

"I am trying to process it all."

"That is a challenge. Especially with so much contradictory information."

She pressed her lips together and looked to the side. Had he erred in his words? He didn't mean to challenge what she thought. But he did wish she didn't accept everything she heard as fact. For so much of it was speculation and rhetoric...what wasn't intentionally meant to elicit fear.

"I just mean that I have had a hard time, too...trying to decide what is true and who to trust."

The muscles around her mouth eased and she looked at him again. "What...what are we supposed to do about the wedding?"

They had not ventured there yet. Mostly because he didn't want to. Was she reluctant as well? It didn't seem so.

"There is no reason to do anything right now. Let's see how all this turns out. It may be over in a month."

"You think so?" It was clear she was rather skeptical.

He sighed. "I don't know. I wish I did."

She offered him a slight smile. "At least we can agree on that."

"Hey," he said, a mock reprimand. "So we agree I don't know."

"Sounds about right." Now her lips widened.

He slapped a hand over his heart, but he beamed at her. "Ouch."

She fingered the collar of her shirt and he tried not to think about how much he wanted to encase her hand in his. How he longed to kiss her full lips. That would only grow a hunger in him that could not be sated.

"It's good to see you smile," he admitted. "I have missed your laugh."

She nodded. "Me too."

Did she mean she had missed her own laughter? Or his?

He opted not to go there. He may not like the answer.

"I, um, need to get these groceries wiped down." She looked offscreen at something to the side again.

Wiped down? She was wiping the groceries down? That struck him as a little excessive. But he dare not judge.

"Okay." He hoped he kept the sadness from his voice, but that didn't seem likely. Not based on her reaction.

"But I want you to call me when you get home," she was quick to say.

"Call? Or FaceTime?" He had enjoyed these moments too much to go back to just her voice.

She smiled. "We can FaceTime."

"Good." He let out a breath. "I love you."

"I love you more." It was music to his ears.

"No," he shot back.

"Yes...now get going!" She giggled.

He watched as she blew him a kiss and then ended the connection.

As he backed his car out of the parking space, he felt a little more whole. That was the most he'd seen of her in a week. He hadn't realized just how starved for her he had become. And it had been a piece of heaven.

# reunited

6 April 1918

Dr. Hendry,

I thank you for your updates. Though I am sad to hear that no more information has come to light. We are struggling still. Hoping against hope that your work will shine a light on something that may help...

T heodore tucked the letter back into his jacket pocket as the train lurched once more. He couldn't decide if he were more bothered to be pulled from his research to lend his aid as a physician or more excited at the prospect of seeing Rose again.

The powers that be at Fort Campbell had opted to send him back to Fort Riley as a measure of reinforcement for the growing number of sick. Though they still refused to see eye-to-eye with him about what to share with the populace.

Scanning the passengers around him, he swallowed his horror

at the way they went about their lives, oblivious to the danger they faced every time they sat next to a stranger. Or even a loved one, at that.

His gaze caught on the woman two rows up. She rode with a man and a child, who snuggled close to her side. But the thing that had drawn his attention was her cough. It was what he would consider a dry cough. It could be allergies or some manner of mild cold. Or something more nefarious.

He would be a fool to think that the illness that plagued Fort Riley had not spread elsewhere. As quickly as it moved among those in the camp and surrounding area, he would wager it had found victims all over the country. Or soon would.

The woman coughed again and leaned forward, even as she pressed a hand to her child.

His heart hurt to think that she might carry the strain of flu that had claimed many lives already. Even more, she may be passing it onto her more vulnerable child. Though, was that the case? More of the infected and dying had been in this woman's age category than in the child's — contrary to most influenzas and counter to what one would expect. Perhaps that was due more to the fact that the majority of individuals on the Camp Funston base were in their twenties and thirties. Or did this flu truly afflict the relatively young adults in such a skewed fashion?

It was difficult to know without more information. And that, he was not likely to get with newspapers and news casting on the radio suppressing the information on this health crisis. Blast it! He hated that his superior officers rendered even him impotent to help in this way.

What could be gained by this family in front of him if they were informed? If the woman knew to seek out care sooner rather than later?

The woman coughed again and then struggled to regain her breath.

Her daughter maneuvered until she could see her mother's face. "Mama, what's wrong?"

Theodore wished he could snatch the child back and somehow prevent further risk of the girl contracting the illness, but he was paralyzed by his duty to his superiors.

Indeed, he couldn't be certain the woman carried the foul disease.

The individuals around her didn't pay much heed to her— neither to distance themselves nor bother with the noise. Such was the hustle and bustle of transit.

Her husband pulled out his handkerchief and offered it to her as he set an arm around her. He pressed a hand to her face. "You are burning up."

"It's nothing," she choked out as she fought to contain another fit of coughing.

Before he realized it, Theodore was on his feet and moving toward the small family.

As much as he wanted to help the woman, there was no treatment he had run across that would calm the influenza as it moved through her body. In fact, she may not make it to see the next day, if it was the flu they fought at Fort Riley. Even young adults fell to the flu in a matter of hours.

He slid into the row behind the family and leaned toward the husband, careful to keep from breathing deeply. As if that could stop the sickness. If this was the same influenza as the one spreading in Kansas, likely everyone in this car was vulnerable.

"Sir, I do ask your pardon..." Theodore opted to pull out his own handkerchief and cover his nose and mouth. There were a couple of odd glances in his direction, but he didn't care. "I'm a doctor. And I think your wife needs to isolate."

"Isolate?" the man spoke loud enough to make Theodore cringe and to draw more onlookers.

Theodore smiled and waved his free hand in a dismissive way

but then remembered he covered his mouth and no one could see his attempt to ease them.

"Yes, sir. I think it would be best if you go home and keep her to a separate bedroom until she has recovered."

The man turned a wide-eyed gaze on Theodore. "Are you crazy? It's just a cold."

Theodore bit at his lower lip, caught in indecision. "Perhaps."

"What are you saying?" the man pressed, glancing to his wife and then to Theodore.

What could he say? He dare not violate the direct order issued to him. But wasn't his responsibility to these people, his calling as a doctor, and his duty as a Christian caring for his neighbor more important?

"Well?" The man scoffed. Gone was the hint of fear that had been in his eyes. Now, the man seemed rather belligerent. "Are you trying to scare us?"

Theodore dropped his gaze. "No..." Yet he hesitated to continue.

"I will thank you to return to your seat and leave my family alone." The man turned away but shot sideways glances at Theodore.

Theodore shook his head. How could he go on without doing all he could? But in his mind's eye, he imagined sharing just what he knew. And the possible panic that would ensue in this train car and everywhere these people went.

It did tempt him, but such a panic was not the answer either.

Still, he could not remain quiet. "I beg you, sir, just do it. If I'm crazy, it has cost you nothing but a few nights away from your wife. If I'm not crazy, it may save you. And your daughter."

The man's steely gaze landed on Theodore once more. But there was a layer of fear underneath.

Theodore prayed both that the man would expose this little bit of information to the whole car in a loud outburst and that he would just believe and remain quiet. Which did Theodore want more?

The man gave him a long, hard look and repeated, "Leave my family alone."

Theodore nodded and rose, defeat falling on his shoulders. But he could hope that the man might think on the words exchanged here and heed the advice. At least Theodore could pray he would.

He did not remove his handkerchief from his own face until he had moved to the far side of the car. But this he knew—he could not be out in the world and remain silent.

Rose settled onto a chair. She had not sat in several hours. At least not since breakfast. How much longer would this grueling work press her? She pulled the latest letter from Theodore out of her apron. Why she found comfort in it, she did not know. Whether or not she should, that was a question better left unanswered. For the guilt lying underneath it was as a storm about to brew. It was best she not tempt it. For she may just come unraveled if she did.

Opening the folds of the pages, she glanced over the contents.

*Dear Rose,*

*I know you are acquainted with the measures of the war. The country presses on with all it has to join the fight. But I remain concerned about the spread of this disease. While many recover, the death toll speaks to me as well. If only there were a better answer. The movement of troops for war also means a wider spread for this sickness. And the tight quarters soldiers find themselves in...it cannot be good for halting the progression of this horrid plague...*

"Nurse Garrett," a voice called to her, pulling her from the draw of Theodore's words.

Before she sought the face of whomever beseeched her, her weariness swelled. Was it never enough? Would it ever be?

Another nurse had stepped into the only quiet space in the whole of the camp—the mess hall. At least, it was quiet when it wasn't mealtime. And all the more so as there were fewer soldiers well enough to indulge in such pleasantries.

"What is it?" Rose pulled from deep within, trying to gather the strength to go back into the fray.

"Dr. Donovan requests your presence."

Rose sighed. There was something to be said for being the most experienced nurse at the base. Then again, it laid a lot of responsibility on her.

She shoved the letter back into her apron pocket and stood. "Coming."

The kind, but young nurse smiled and moved off.

Rose tucked her hair behind her ear, what of it had come loose, and moved toward the medical ward. Dr. Donovan wouldn't have summoned her unless it was important. Surely the man knew how long she had been laboring—patting down feverish brows and bodies, administering aspirin, and tending the ill.

Soon enough, she entered the overfull room and scanned for the doctor. He leaned over a patient across the room.

Walking around cots, she made her way there. The ward used to have direct paths between the rows of beds, but so many additional cots had to be procured that floor space was at a premium.

Shaking her head, she opted to consider that later. She strode to the doctor's side and waited for him to notice her.

After some moments, she cleared her throat.

Only then did he turn. "Nurse Garrett."

"Yes, doctor?"

"I couldn't determine how long ago this man's dose was." He held out a clipboard to her. "I can't even make out the name of the dispensing nurse."

The handwriting was indeed scrawled out and illegible. She looked for the nurse's name, hoping for better luck discerning it.

"Dr. Donovan, this was Nurse Galston's patient." Rose frowned. The woman was unreliable in the best of circumstances.

"Ah...shall we find the woman then?"

"Unfortunately, sir," the other, younger nurse spoke up, "She has retired for the evening."

Retired? When did she get such reprieve? Nurse Galston hadn't been on shift until after Rose. It was like a punch to Rose's gut. But she dare not complain. These were tenuous times that required one to overlook grievances and be thankful for life.

The doctor grimaced. He wasn't above having the woman wakened. But he also wasn't one to disturb his resting nurses if he could avoid it. Well, unless it was Rose.

"Give him 400mg of aspirin."

"But..." Rose started, biting her lip to keep the words in. Was there risk of overdosing the man? There was much still not known about aspirin. Besides, that seemed like a lot for them to not know how much was in his system.

Dr. Donovan's eyebrows lifted. "Yes?"

She dropped her gaze to the floor. "Yes, doctor." Questioning him would get her nowhere. This was Dr. Donovan's call and his responsibility. But she couldn't shake her culpability in her silent assent.

He nodded to the young nurse beside Rose, who reached for the bottle.

"Walk with me." He indicated that Rose should follow.

She did so, not looking forward to what might be coming.

They went past the mish mosh of cots and through to a mostly vacant room before he turned toward her.

"These nurses all look up to you." His eyes were hard, but the lines about them belied his fatigue.

She nodded. Though she had never asked for nor wanted to be lauded or idolized in any way.

"I need you to trust me." Dr. Donovan was resolute, but his tone bordered on being dismissive of her.

"Yes, doctor. I do."

An eyebrow piqued.

"You know I do."

He sighed and nodded. "I think it's time you gain your rest. You've been here since sun up."

At least someone noticed. She offered the best smile she could muster. "Thank you, doctor."

She moved past him and out of the building. Her bunk was nothing to be praised, but she longed for it in that moment. Just a few hours' rest before she faced more of the same again. Wrapping her arms about herself, she hoped to ward off the chill. Not from the air, but from within. The task that lay before her everyday was impossible. And yet somehow she plugged on. Because people relied on her. Because she had to.

"Rose?" a voice called from her right.

She spun even as she believed she knew who owned the voice. It was familiar and yet not at the same time. As she turned, her eyes confirmed what everything else in her hoped. Hoped?

Theodore Hendry.

"Is it really you?" Emotion caught in her throat. Had she, in her fatigue, conjured him? He was in Fort Campbell, so many miles away, trying to find answers for this illness that ravaged the state.

"Yes." He moved toward her, as if drawn by some unseen force. Truly it was her imagination.

Should she step closer? How did one behave with a mirage? Especially one that was welcomed.

She pressed the guilt that swelled to the side. Not now.

He stood just an arm's length from her. "Are you well?" His concern emanated off him as if he radiated it.

She shook her head, unable to find the words. Then she stepped closer and leaned toward him.

Without resistance, he wrapped his arms about her.

Tears rolled down her face, and exhaustion threatened to overcome her. But she found comfort in his surprisingly solid arms.

As she clung to him, something seemed strange. She wanted to put it out of mind and relish this moment, but it nagged. Turning to the side, she spotted it again—a suitcase.

Suitcase? Why would she imagine such a thing?

Then she realized—a thought that was both elating and disheartening at the same time—he really was here.

Jerking away from him, she tried to pull herself together.

His brow furrowed and he seemed even more concerned. "What is it? Are you all right?"

She nodded, slapping at the tears on her cheeks. "Yes, Dr. Hendry, I am just fine. Although I...must apologize for my behavior."

He set a hand to her shoulder. "Believe me, there is nothing to apologize for."

She dared to meet his gaze again. His affect spoke to the sincerity of his words.

"There is no need."

"I..." She wanted to repeat her apology. Or hide. Or something...

He set tentative hands to her arms. "Tell me."

She looked away, unable to bear the care in his gaze anymore. "Forgive me, I'm overtired."

His hands slid away. She regretted their absence immediately. But it couldn't be because of this. That's not what this was. It had been a friendly correspondence. Nothing more.

But as her heart tugged at his obvious disappointment, she knew it was more.

"I...need to gain my bed." She braved looking at him.

He nodded. "As well you should. I have other things to attend to myself."

She shifted and moved off without another word. But she felt his gaze on her the entirety of her walk until she was out of sight.

# EIGHT

*facades*

*April 17, 2020*
*Wyngate Apartments*
*Cordova, TN*

Brianne sat at her desk. She had finally showered, due in no small part to her parents' insistence on talking through video conferencing so they could see her. It had been drudgery to do so after so many days of skipping.

Still, she had done it. For her own benefit as much as for her parents. She couldn't manage them demanding she come home. Or check into a mental hospital because she was not taking care of herself. *Sheesh!*

Sucking in a breath, she clicked on the Zoom link and waited.

There was no reason to expect that her parents could operate the Zoom website. Then again, this shelter-at-home brought about more know-how with technology than she'd have thought.

Still, she waited.

The square for her parents popped up, but a torso was all she saw. And then she heard her sister's voice.

"You have to uncover your camera. Honestly, dad, are you so afraid the government is watching you around the clock?"

Brianne snickered in spite of herself.

Her sister's face appeared as she leaned away from the laptop. And Brianne's parents were doing their best to see around Lori's moving figure.

"I can't see!" Mom said, her tone somewhat harsh.

"Because I'm not out of the way yet," Lori groused. "For the love!"

Brianne suppressed another giggle. She missed her family so much. They were a light in this dark time. They always were. Even Lori...with all their differences over the last several years...they had just started to become closer. Then this happened.

"Hey, Lori," Brianne called out before her sister could back away.

"Hey," Lori said on a sigh. "How are you?"

Brianne nodded at her sister's face on the screen even as she fought tears. The sadness at being separated from them overwhelmed her more than she'd thought it would.

"You okay, sweetheart?" Mom's face appeared beside Lori's.

"Yeah. I'm just...so happy to see you." Brianne swallowed past the lump forming in her throat.

"Then I can't imagine why you won't come home." That was Mom...always cutting to the chase. Well...often.

"I just don't feel safe about the three-hour drive." That's what she'd been telling herself. "Having to stop for gas and stuff. There are so many germs on those gas pumps. And what if I have to go to the bathroom...it would be a nightmare." Even saying it brought anxiety crashing down on her.

"Oh, that's nonsense." Dad's voice came from behind Lori. "There's no need to be afraid. These COVID germs were around months ago and you were going to gas pumps and gas station bathrooms then."

Brianne nodded but didn't really want to give his words credence. That was then. Now she knew better. What was it Mom always said? God helps those who help themselves? It didn't seem exactly theologically sound, but it worked for this instance.

Lori held up a hand in a wave-like gesture. "I'll let you all chat. Text me later, sis."

Brianne nodded and watched as Lori moved out of the way and her father's larger frame became visible. Then Brianne delved into the screen-rendered images of her parents. Even with their quirks and sometimes unreasonable demands, she loved them. They were her parents. And she missed them.

But not enough to risk what she'd have to in order to come home.

"What are you doing to keep yourself from sleeping all day? Can't be easy in that small apartment." Mom seemed able to see past the camera and stare right at Brianne. Was she watching for any sign of faltering?

"I have work. And there's always the judge shows."

Dad laughed.

Mom did not. She frowned and said, "Oh goodness. You can't mean that."

As a fact, Brianne meant it more than she dared express. Things were a bit lonely. And tiresome. At first, she'd had all this time to get stuff done. Catch up on all the house stuff. And even indulge in a few hobbies. Now, it felt useless.

"Don't worry, just about the time I get sucked in, the governor breaks into the show and shares all the things he feels he needs to say."

Dad frowned. "I think he's doing the best he can."

"I know that. I'm just teasing."

"There are a lot of people who think the president should do more. But I think he is also doing the best he can." Dad folded his arms.

Dad had always been a big fan of the president. It wasn't as if Brianne believed he could do better, but there were plenty who thought so. She'd only seen one picture with him wearing a mask. And while she wanted to believe he was taking the same measures he asked of the country, she didn't know who to believe.

"I think that's all anyone can do." Brianne tried to remain neutral. "The best they can with the information they have."

"And do we get a lot of that." Mom spoke up. "There is so much. Masks work, masks don't do anything. We need vaccinations, we need natural immunity...on and on."

"Yeah. It's crazy." Brianne really didn't want to spend her time on Zoom with her parents talking about this. "What are y'all doing these days?"

"Your dad keeps making a mess of the yard with that backhoe."

"I need to get that line fixed."

"So he says." Mom directed this to Brianne. "I wish he'd call someone."

"Really? With the coronavirus out there? You want some stranger coming to the house?" Brianne couldn't imagine it. Maybe she was much better off staying here.

"Well..." Mom started.

"I can handle it," Dad said with finality.

Mom held up a hand. "At least it keeps you busy. I'm just thankful for grocery pick up and online deliveries."

Again, Brianne couldn't imagine an influx of packages covered with unknown germs. "I hope you're staying safe."

"Of course we are," Mom shot back, not in a harsh way, but in a firm way. "We keep doing what we're supposed to."

Brianne would just have to trust that they were. She couldn't control them. Never in a million years. Her parents were the very definition of stubborn.

Brianne's phone buzzed. She pulled it out to check the screen.

"What is that?" Mom's curiosity got the better of her.

"It's just Scott trying to FaceTime me."

"Oh, you and your fancy phones." Mom smiled.

Brianne hit the cancel button and sent Scott a quick text that she was on a call with her parents.

"Do you need to get that?" Dad leaned toward the screen as if he could come through to her apartment.

"No. I'm talking to you two right now. I'll call him back."

"It's okay. You can call him now. We can catch up later." Mom beamed. "Now that we've got this infernal thing figured out."

Brianne nodded. "Are you sure?"

"Yeah. Tell that future son-in-law of mine that he owes me a Face-thingy." Dad grinned.

"It's a FaceTime. And you have to have an iPhone to do that."

"Oh...what's this thing on the computer then?"

How were her parents so tech inept? They lived in a high speed age of technological development. But they had never really cared to keep up, so they didn't. With Dad running his own business, it wasn't imperative they maintain their technology if they didn't want to.

And Lori was always close at hand. That may not always be the case. She would graduate in a year. If this COVID thing settled and allowed her to.

"It's called video conferencing," Brianne offered.

"I'll never remember that." Dad frowned.

"Zoom. It's a Zoom call." Brianne hoped that might be easier.

Dad waved her off. "Go call Scott. Let me get back to my work in the yard."

"Oh no you won't," Mom spoke up. "I've got a few things for you to take care of around here."

Brianne smiled again. This was her parents. And she had not realized how much she needed to see their bickering. It was all in love, so it was a comfort.

When the lump in her throat threatened again, she waved to get their attention. "Hey!"

They looked her way.

"I'm going to let y'all go."

"How do we hang up on this thing?" Mom reached for the keyboard, and Brianne heard a couple of clicks. "Does this—?" And then the screen went black.

Shaking her head, she smiled. What else could she expect?

Nothing else.

Nor did she want for something more or less than they really were. In fact, their inability to change soothed her worn nerves quite a bit.

*April 17, 2020*
*Trammel Apartments*
*Cordova, TN*

Scott lay back on the bed, holding his phone to his chest. He was glad Brianne was on with her parents. It could only be good for her, right? Maybe they'd even convince her to come home for the remainder of this lockdown. As much as he'd hate her being so far away, it would be better for her. Besides, for all the contact they were able to have, she might as well be a million miles away.

His phone rang. Had she hung up on her parents to chat with him? That would not surprise him, but he hated to pull her away.

But as he lifted his phone to answer, a Murfreesboro number flashed on the screen. He hit the green button.

"Hello?"

"Hello. Mr. Baker?" a feminine voice said.

"Yes. Speaking." Who was this? The voice sounded familiar. But most voices blended together through the phone speaker.

"This is Rochelle, from Cherry Lane Inn in Murfreesboro."

"Oh." The wedding venue. What could they be calling to say?

"Unfortunately, because of the shelter-at-home ordinance, we will have to cancel your wedding date."

This was not unexpected, but Scott had not wanted to acknowledge it. Still, this was where they were. He forced a response past the tightness in his chest. "I understand. What are our options?"

"Because of the state of things, we are not currently rebooking. But as soon as things are...safer, you can apply your funds toward another date if you so choose."

Scott didn't know what to say. How would he broach this subject with Brianne? How would she react? How exactly did he feel about the prospect of postponing their wedding staring him in the face?

"Again, unfortunately, we don't have protocols in place for a full cancellation at this point. So, I can't say with confidence what will happen to your deposit if that is the case."

He nodded then remembered she couldn't see him. "Yes, I understand. I will need to talk with my fiancée and get back to you."

"Of course, Mr. Baker. We look forward to hearing from you."

"Thanks." Scott pulled the phone away from his ear and hit the end call button. As he did so, he noticed that he had missed a call.

Scrolling over to that screen, he spied Brianne's number. Was he ready to have this conversation about the wedding venue now? He wasn't sure he needed to lay more on her plate.

He set the phone down and sat up. It wasn't that he wanted to keep things from her, but he wanted to protect her...especially right now. It was then decided, if she brought it up, he would be honest, but there was little reason for him to mention it off hand.

Swiping over to his contacts, he pressed on Brianne's name and then hit the FaceTime button.

The phone rang with him staring at himself for a minute.

Then she appeared, and his image moved to a small square in the corner.

"Hey." He wished, yet again, that he could reach through to her. She looked...better somehow. More refreshed. And her hair had been done. It had been a while since he'd seen it in anything but a ponytail. And...had she applied makeup?

"Hey. Just finished with my parents." Brianne smiled. "They are a pair for sure."

"That they are," Scott agreed. He could only imagine them trying to manage the video conferencing. "Did they figure out Zoom?" That was a dumb question. For her to have chatted with them, they must have.

"Lori had to help. But they managed to hang up on me."

He laughed. That sounded about right.

"Do you need to call them back?" He didn't want to keep her.

"No. We were done."

He grinned. "How was it?"

"It was...good to talk to them. Of course, they tried to tell me I needed to come home."

He nodded, waiting.

"They just don't understand. They aren't nervous about all the places this virus can lurk."

"Hmmm." What could he say to that? He didn't agree with her fears, but he didn't want it to seem as if he didn't support her.

"So, what have you got going on today?"

He was glad she changed the subject. "Coding."

"Ah...no rest for the weary?"

"Yep. Whether good or bad, my job doesn't need a cubicle to

get done. Makes me wonder why they insist we maintain an office anyway."

"Come on, you'd miss the interaction with your co-workers, and you know it."

"Yeah, I guess you're right."

She smirked. "You *guess* I'm right? How about you know it?"

"Okay..." He held up his hands in a mock surrender. "You're right...you always have been right and you always will be right."

She beamed then. "Just remember that. It will serve you well."

He sighed, enjoying the back and forth. As if nothing had ever happened. Except...she was on a phone screen, not in front of him. "What would I do without you?"

"I don't think you'll have to find out."

Something told him that now was the time to share about the earlier phone call from Cherry Lane Inn. But he didn't want to ruin the moment. "You doing anything fun today?"

"Yeah...I guess. I have been meaning to get my sketchpad out and see if there are any critters or flowers I can capture from the back." She indicated something in front of her as if he could see where she pointed.

"That sounds like fun. You'll have to snap a picture for me when you're done."

She chewed on her bottom lip.

"Come on, Brie. Don't make me come over there," he joked.

Her face went blank. And he realized. That was a bit too far.

"Brie, I didn't mean..."

She shook her head. "I knew what you meant."

"Sorry...I didn't mean to bring the mood down."

"It's okay." Her eyes told a very different story. "I need to get going anyway."

"Brie, I—"

"It's not because of what you said. I just...have some things to get done."

He knew that wasn't the whole truth, but he would have to let her have space as she needed it. No matter how it sliced through him to let her go. "Okay. Talk later?"

She nodded. And then the screen went dark.

How could he continue like this? It was an emotional roller coaster. *Somehow*, he told himself, *I will. No...we will.*

*April 22, 2020*
*Wyngate Apartments*
*Cordova, TN*

Brianne settled into the chair behind her desk. Why were these chairs so cheap? Well, that was partly her choice, wasn't it? When buying things for the apartment, she did not feel like splurging on a better desk chair was worth it. With her being at this desk so much this last month though, she was reconsidering that decision.

Her eyes wandered over the hutch looming over her computer. She did love her knick knacks and pictures—no one could look at her desk and not realize that. The shelves were full of memories— some fun, most pleasant. But when she set her gaze on the cross that Latasha had gifted her after her near attempt on her own life, her smile fell. Those mental images were dark, but there was hope. God had surely saved her from herself.

She shook off a shudder at that and clicked to open the Zoom window. Rainbow wheel. Grrr.

Soon enough, however, a window popped up indicating the host would let her in soon. Glancing at her laptop screen clock, she noted that it was a few minutes before her session.

What would her counselor say about the current situation? About Brianne's current situation?

It was no surprise that Scott did not totally approve of her choices...and her fears. But he didn't have to walk in her skin. Though...perhaps he was right. Maybe.

She shivered and looked down at her arms as they wrapped around her chest. The skin of her arms was scabbed from her picking. What would Sheri say about that? Not that Brianne had to tell her. If she kept her arms down, the woman wouldn't be able to see them. Maybe she should go grab a cardigan for good measure.

Even as she started to rise, she stopped herself. It would not serve her to hide it. Sheri was always compassionate without being soft. Exactly what Brianne needed—someone who would call her on the lies she told herself and the excuses she often made.

The window on the screen widened and the turning blue circle within gave Brianne something to focus on while she drew in a breath and let it out.

Soon enough, Sheri's face appeared in the box next to Brianne's. Without hesitation, Brianne clicked the setting button and hid her own view. Then only Sheri was on her screen. No sense in being distracted making sure she looked okay in her image.

"Good morning!" Sheri smiled. "It's been a few weeks."

The words were not harsh, but a firm unspoken reminder. Brianne caught it well enough and nodded. "I've been busy."

"Have you?" Again Sheri's lilting voice took the sting out of the question.

Brianne smiled despite the tightness in her chest. She pushed out a breath and stretched her arms, trying to bring some ease to the shakiness.

"What have you been up to?" Sheri was never one for rabbit trails. Always right to the point.

"I've had work for the center. Calling clients and whatnot."

Sheri nodded but did not speak.

"And I've been staying in touch with my parents and Latasha and Scott."

"How is everyone?"

"Good. My parents want me to come home."

"And you don't want to?"

"I...don't know how I feel about the drive and having to stop along the way."

"I see. It's always good to be cautious."

Should Brianne share that Latasha had also offered a guest room to her? Brianne had no legitimate excuses for refusing that, other than her anxiety about more risk. Was that valid though? It felt real.

Brianne tugged the hair at the side of her face behind both ears.

"What happened to your arm?" Sheri's voice was not judging or accusing. Just curious.

"I...have been picking my skin."

"Oh?"

"Yes. I find that the idle time makes me itch."

"Hmmm...have you tried keeping something in your hands? Like one of your crochet projects?"

"No. I...haven't felt much like doing any of that."

"Well, even if you just fiddle around with it, why don't you try picking that up whenever you're watching television or just sitting around chatting. It may make a difference."

Brianne offered her a smile. Again, she appreciated that Sheri was just easy with her. "I'll pull it out and give that a try."

Sheri grinned. "That's all I ask."

Silence fell between them. Their last several sessions before the lockdown had been more conversational. Now, Brianne felt uncertain of what to say. It concerned her about herself.

Sheri broke the silence. "How is Scott?"

"He's good. I think he'd prefer I find somewhere to go and not be alone here." Brianne couldn't help the dryness that seeped into her voice.

"I'm sensing a pattern here."

Brianne held her breath.

Sheri ventured a thought. "What do *you* think?"

"I...am getting into a rhythm here. I don't want to reinvent the wheel."

Sheri's eyes became serious. "I get that. How are you managing your daily things?"

"I am cleaning daily and making sure to shower and eat." Well, she had only showered twice this month—once before her call with her parents and before this call. But she decided it was true enough.

"Cleaning daily? Like...the apartment?"

"Yeah. I find it keeps me busy and sane."

"I have no doubt it fills your time. But I am curious...what do you mean when you say it keeps you sane?"

*Uh oh.* Why had she said that? She wanted to kick herself. Though...this was a safe place. And she needed, more than anything, to be able to be honest here. "I...have been a bit more... concerned...about the germs floating around this complex. That's not too far out there, I think. I am following the guidelines about staying put, but I don't know what the other tenants are doing."

"True." Sheri shrugged. "But you're worried that the coronavirus is somehow able to get into your apartment." It wasn't a question.

"Maybe." Brianne felt less sure about her trepidation. "But I can't not worry about it."

"You know, one of the important things I like to say is that you don't have to think every thought that comes into your head."

"Huh." Brianne had heard this, but it always took her a second. It was true though. Just because she had a thought, didn't mean she had to dwell on it, nurse it, let it have its own train in her head.

"Are you good on groceries and the essentials?"

"Yeah. Scott does a porch drop off when I need things."

"That's nice. What do you do when he does that?"

"I..." Should she admit this? "I...wipe them down."

Sheri only nodded. "I can understand that. A lot of people are in that same place. Are you watching the regular news updates?"

"How can I miss them? They are constantly on."

"You may need to be mindful of how much information you're taking in. There is a real danger of information overload. And that can be heavy."

Brianne hadn't considered that. It was only prudent to be on top of the most recent news, right? But Scott kept saying it wasn't all trustworthy. How was she supposed to weed out what was and wasn't good information? Shouldn't she err on the side of caution?

"You seem to be thinking," Sheri cut in.

"It's just that..." Brianne blew out a breath. "Well, Scott says the same kind of thing. He thinks I put too much stock in everything I'm hearing from the CDC and the local news."

"Well, it's a balance, I think. There is a lot of information and there is wisdom in being in the know. But for your own mental health, I think you should limit it. Maybe pick one or two news sources—perhaps reliable online places...and keep to just that."

Brianne nodded, knowing that this would be more challenging than remembering to get her crochet stuff when she was idle.

"Just give it a try," Sheri encouraged. Did she see Brianne's doubt?

Of course she did.

But how could Brianne fight herself in these things? The need to know was real. The anxiety was real. The fear was real.

"Tell me about what you're doing for fun. Pulled out your sketchbook yet?"

"Yeah. Not seeing much inspiring me from the back door. It's like the animals understand what I'm doing and try to stay away until I put the paper away. Then they're running wild back there."

"You have a screened in porch, right?"

"It's Memphis. I don't know why it wouldn't be screened in."

Sheri laughed a little. "Well, take some coffee out there and just sit with the fresh air."

Brianne balked. She couldn't help it. The only way to keep the COVID germs out was to keep her apartment shut up, right? She risked enough opening the door for groceries.

"I've already given you a couple of things to try out. So, why don't you just think about this porch thing?"

Brianne gave a hesitant nod. That she could do. Though she was sure she was certain how those thoughts would go.

"Before we close this, I want to get you on my schedule for next week."

"Next week?" Brianne had reached the point she was seeing Sheri every other week. Why next week?

"I am trying to see my clients every week for a little bit. Those that can. It's a unique time with unique challenges. And I am starting to see the beginnings of a mental health crisis for many. I want to ward that off as much as possible. It's just a precaution."

Brianne nodded, slowly. "Okay. What do you have open?"

"I have your regular time—Wednesdays at 10am. Does that work?"

Brianne had the thought that she should check her schedule. But what would be on there? Nothing. "That will work."

She grabbed her phone and punched in the appointment as Sheri clicked keys on her keyboard...probably doing the same thing.

"Take care. And give those things a try." Sheri's eyes softened. She really did understand. Or at least tried to.

Brianne was thankful for her. They had walked a long journey together after Brianne's release from the mental hospital following her near attempt. And she had come a long way. She had come too far, and labored for each bit of progress...to let this overwhelm her.

She refused to let the coronavirus rob her of that. She could do this.

## NINE

# *contemplating*

*April 10, 1918*

*Dearest Mother,*

*Though I had my fears and doubts, the illness seems to be abating. If only slightly. But every little bit is a big thing for us. We have been pushed and overwhelmed for so long. Though, having Dr. Hendry here has been a piece of heaven.*

Rose paused. A piece of heaven? Why would she write that? It seemed almost as if he meant more to her than he should. That was something her mother certainly wouldn't understand. Perhaps not even appreciate. Her courtship and engagement to Walter had happened quickly. But he had been important to her. She had planned to marry him, for goodness' sake. She couldn't just dismiss that...not for some random feelings nor for this attraction to Theodore.

There she went again. She needed to remember propriety. He

was Dr. Hendry to her. Nothing more than a colleague and perhaps acquaintance.

But she knew better. He had become more. The minute they started exchanging letters. The second she poured her heart out to him. And the moment she let herself be enfolded in his embrace.

Her face heated as she remembered that moment of weakness. Not that she hadn't dwelt on it...often. She had. She let herself dream on it and take comfort in the warmth of the memory. Even that had to stop.

"What are you thinking on so heavily?" Another young nurse came into the barracks, walking around Rose to get to her own cot.

"Nothing." Rose covered the letter with her arm. That would be unforgiveable...if the other nurses found out about her thoughts of Theodore...er, Dr. Hendry. What would they think of her?

Likely that she was a shallow woman, trying to gain the inside track and that she was heartless toward Walter's memory.

The other nurse shrugged and landed on her cot. "What a day!"

"Indeed." Rose turned back to her letter, now that it was well out of range of the young woman. "Are you done for the day?"

She nodded. "Aren't you?"

"I have a few patients to check on. So, almost done."

"I don't know how you do it. You're up earlier than everyone else. You stay late in the medical ward. And you barely take time to eat."

Rose frowned. Was that true? And was it so noticeable to others?

"You need to take care," the woman warned. "I've seen many nurses earn nothing more than contracting an illness for such effort."

Rose considered that but said out loud, "I'll give it some thought."

"I can't blame you though. That Dr. Hendry is handsome."

"Oh?" Rose shot a look at the girl. Could she know what Rose had been thinking? Or was there some other clue? No, that was preposterous.

But wait...if this wasn't about Rose, then that would mean this nurse had an interest in Theodore.

"Yes. Those blue eyes are so dreamy." The younger woman rolled over in her bed to face Rose. "And his dark hair...thick and wavy. Have mercy!"

Rose pursed her lips. Yes, he was handsome. She would have had to be blind not to notice. Was her attraction to him all about his physical appearance? That thought bothered. It wasn't as if she were just interested in the physical things about love. But the heat creeping into her cheeks definitely belied that this was at least partly true. After all, she wasn't denying the attraction. Just the depth and reasonableness of it.

Either way, she wasn't sure she liked this woman drooling over him.

"Don't act like you haven't noticed," the girl said. "I've seen you staring at him."

The heat deepened in intensity. How could she deny it? "Perhaps. We still have to keep things professional. We're in the middle of a crisis."

There. If that didn't shame some sense into this woman...and into her own response...maybe nothing would.

The girl shrugged. "Have it your way. But if he looked at me the way he looks at you, I'd be wanting him to do more than play doctor and nurse."

Rose speared her with another look. The audacity! Why would she be thinking such a thing? At a time like this?

But the thought crept unbidden into Rose's awareness...could it be true? Did Theodore look at her some special way? And if so, what was she to do about it?

Theodore signed off on his last chart of the day and glanced across the room. Most everyone had retired for the night. Only one nurse sat at a cot on the other side of the room. He knew before she turned that it was Rose. She was so dedicated to her patients. Often, she was the last one in the ward for the evening.

It warmed his heart and saddened him at the same time. For her to truly care that way meant that the previous patients lost to her had injured that tender heart.

What would it be like for her to feel so toward him? It was not the first time he wondered such. But it always brought his mind back to that night earlier in the week when she had stepped into his embrace. It had more than heated his core to have her in his arms. And as she removed herself, it left an ache he had not been able to shake free of.

Perhaps she was the only answer for it.

He shook his head. That was ridiculous. What an overemotional man this plague had created in him. For surely that's what it was. That's when it had started...on his last visit to Fort Riley. When he first met Rose.

*Stop it*, he admonished himself. This was going nowhere. Rose had just lost her fiancé. And she had made it fairly clear that she was not interested in pursuing anything romantic yet. Not that there was room to consider it in the midst of this madness.

Then why did his feet carry him across the room to her position?

As he neared, he heard her release a shaky sigh. Was she fighting those softer emotions that made her a great nurse?

The man whose bedside she had planted herself at had struggled this day. Though he was Dr. Donovan's patient, Theodore had known. Agitation, fever, wheezing, convulsions, and confusion had all been visited upon him. And Rose remained by his side throughout it all. How must her fiancé's death have torn at her if a stranger's undid her like this?

He listened, careful not to make a sound.

She sniffled.

This voyeurism was not right. But how could he let her know he was here without startling her?

He cleared his throat.

She turned, wiping at her eyes. "Theo—Dr. Hendry, I didn't know you were still here."

Then she didn't keep track of him the way he did her, his heart drawn in her direction. "I just finished with my last patient of the day. What is this man's status?"

"He...has slipped into a coma."

Not unusual for those who fought this battle. And none had yet recovered from a sickness-induced coma. If the pattern held, he would slip into death in the next few hours.

"I'm sorry." Indeed he was. So very sorry.

"I...wish I had done more." Her words faded as she turned back toward the man.

"What more could you have done?" His heart hurt for her. "You gave so diligently of yourself."

"What if...?" She stopped herself.

"What if...what?" He moved closer. Now he stood just a pace away.

She looked up at him, her green eyes misty and wide. So vulnerable. So trusting. And a silent war raged within her. It was plain to see. If only he could shield her from whatever bothered her so.

"I...shouldn't say."

Something was very wrong here. Without thinking twice, he

reached down and gently pulled her up to stand in front of him. Then he rubbed his thumb in small circles on her upper arm, offering what comfort he could. What comfort she would permit.

She stood nearly against him, their bodies only separated by an inch. The urge to pull her to himself was overwhelming. But he resisted.

"Please, tell me what is weighing on you." He wanted to support her any way possible and take this burden from her.

She looked away, the battle taking over again.

He lifted her face toward him with a hooked finger on her chin. "You can trust me."

Theodore had never meant anything more.

She pressed out a ragged breath. "I should not have just stood by while Dr. Donovan ordered more aspirin."

"What?" That confused him. It wasn't like her to question Dr. Donovan. What had driven her to do so?

"He...couldn't read the previous nurse's notes. And he ordered more aspirin without knowing the previous dose."

Theodore nodded, continuing to offer strength through his touch. Hoping that she felt it. "Aspirin is very safe. And it is the only thing we have that will help the symptoms of this awful sickness."

She nodded, her shoulders drooping somewhat. Had he sounded as if he were challenging her?

He softened his voice. "What makes you concerned?"

"It just seems that there is a lot we don't know about dosing aspirin. I don't want to risk giving someone too much of anything."

She made a valid point. One he himself had considered. While the aspirin may be helping with symptoms, it did require careful monitoring. Anything could be given in excess amounts.

He nodded. "I understand."

She blew out another breath, this one steadier. "Will you tell Dr. Donovan?"

He furrowed his brow. "Of course not." His gaze wandered over her features and the movement of the lines on her face. Her dark brown hair had been pulled back earlier in the day, now loosened curls framed her face. A desire to feel their softness rushed through him.

But he focused again on her eyes. "No matter what, Rose, you can trust me. With anything."

The strain about her eyes eased then. "Thank you."

He feared she would pull away, but she didn't. Did she need his comfort as much as he needed to give it?

"You care a great deal for your patients." He was in awe of her capacity to do so. Were there no bounds to her consideration? What would it be like to be the focus of her affection?

Theodore moved his hands up and down her arms. Still, she didn't stop him or make a move to pull away.

She nodded. "I do. It's what drew me into nursing."

He smiled. Her green eyes sparkled now. But they soon dulled again.

"I never expected it would be so difficult...losing so many patients."

"I know. I wish I had more answers. For you."

She jerked her gaze to his once more. "For me?"

He swallowed. "I cannot deny that I'm drawn to you."

Her breaths were so shallow that he could scarcely determine that they still came.

"I know I should not think I would have my feelings returned so soon after your fiancé passed. Still, I find reason to hope."

He lifted a hand to graze the side of her face. "Tell me what you feel, Rose."

Her breath caught. Because she thought him bold? Or because his closeness made her feel something?

She licked her lips, which only served to lower his focus to them for a moment before he set his gaze to hers again. "It is true. I...should be mourning Walter. Another attachment should be the last thing on my mind...especially amidst this horrid plague. Still..."

That last word was the most beautiful thing he'd ever heard.

"Yes?" His voice sounded rough even to him.

"I find myself thinking often of you. And hoping you will think of me the same way I think of you."

"And how is that?"

She stood on her toes and pressed her lips to his. It was a moment of pure heaven. Her mouth was soft and inviting. He had to restrain himself from pouring the full force of his regard into that contact. Otherwise, he might overwhelm her.

He wanted the kiss to convey his true feelings, but in a gentle and tender way. So, after a few moments, he pulled back.

There was a question in her eyes. A question that stabbed at him. He couldn't leave her doubting.

So he placed featherlight kisses to her lips, to her cheek, and to her forehead as he tugged her into his embrace. And he held her as if to never let go. Indeed, he prayed he would never have to.

## *together*

April 28, 1918

Dearest Rose,

These last weeks have meant more than I can say. The chance to work alongside you and become more acquainted with you has been life changing for me. You are as equally amazing in your work as you are a treasure to be sought. And I find I am beyond grateful you have allowed me to get to know you...

Rose read the letter again. Theodore was endearing. He supported her and truly cared for her. Their friendship... well, a bit more than friendship...was more than she had expected so soon after losing Walter. But one cannot choose when God moves in their life. And so, she would just be thankful for it.

Setting the paper back in the box she kept under her cot, she secured it and gathered herself. The day was only half over. There were more patients to tend to and more cleaning to be done.

As she slipped into the medical ward, she prepared to do her rounds. The room seemed more spacious as their numbers had changed. Those who were sick no longer outnumbered the care-givers. And they had been able to remove the extra cots. Well, most of them.

Rose took in a breath and let it out. Things had shifted for the better. There were not as many struggling with the Spanish flu. And not nearly as many dying. It made her heart feel lighter.

"Hello, Nurse Garrett," a deep voice said from behind.

She startled, and tingles traveled the length of her spine as she turned. "Dr. Hendry." Raising an eyebrow, she gave a silent warn-ing. They needed to keep things professional while in the ward.

"I need to speak with you for a moment." He indicated the surgical room off to the side.

Was this a ploy to steal a kiss? She wanted to refuse him with a reminder that others relied on them. But another part of her wanted to follow him and get lost in his kiss.

He offered a quizzical look. "You all right?"

"Yes," she said as her face heated. What was she thinking? She waved a hand in the direction he'd earlier pointed to.

Theodore hesitated, then turned to lead her that way, holding the door open for her to pass in front of him.

Why did his presence have to bring out her jitters? She fairly trembled as she moved close enough to feel the warmth coming from his body.

As she stepped farther into the room, he grabbed for her arm and turned her toward him. Then his lips were on hers.

So this was his plan. She wanted to be angry, but she just couldn't be. Not when his embrace felt so perfect.

Soon enough, he pulled back. "Do you know how difficult it is to see you...to be so close...and not touch you?"

She was certain she was blushing. "I know, but we have to keep things in the ward more strictly professional."

"I understand. And I agree."

She smiled and nodded before stepping back from him, though she was very reluctant to do so. No doubt that showed on her features amidst the pink.

He held to her hand, causing her to halt as she turned.

She faced him again, tugging at her hand to free it. "Theodore..."

"I really did have something to talk to you about." Only then did he release her.

"Oh?" She swallowed, immediately not liking his tone.

"Yes." He watched her as she shifted her body toward his once more. "I have heard from my commanding officer. And I've got orders to resume my research."

She frowned. This possibility had loomed over them since there had been a change in the case load. Since the once rapidly spreading flu had calmed. "Will you do so here?"

He shook his head. "They want me back at Fort Campbell."

She looked to the ground. There was no reason to let him see her disappointment. It wasn't as if he wanted to go, was it? "When..." She heard the tremor in her voice, so she cleared her throat. "When do you have to leave?"

"Tomorrow."

Her shoulders fell as the sadness overwhelmed her. More than she had expected. Especially since she had guessed this to be inevitable.

His hand cupped her face, drawing it up toward his. "I wish more than anything that I could stay. Or that you could go with me."

"I wish that, too." How had she developed such an attachment in so short a time span?

"Then you will continue to write me?" His eyes gleamed, hopeful.

"Of course. I'll keep you updated on our progress here, and—"

"I'd be grateful for that, but I want to continue getting to know *you*."

She let the corners of her mouth curve upward. Then, this wasn't the end of a short-lived romance. He was serious about pursuing her.

He leaned forward and brushed his lips against her cheek before straightening and dropping his arms to his sides. "I can't tell you how glad I am that this flu didn't turn into what I had feared it would be."

The memories of so many lost—Walter, Aubrey, and others—crossed through her mind as if playing on a screen.

"Not that the losses don't matter." He was quick to amend. "They do."

She nodded, letting his presence comfort and soothe her wounded heart.

"But it could have been much worse. It should have been." His conviction stirred her.

"You're right. We should be thankful for what grace is given us." She allowed the truth of that statement to penetrate the grief-stricken places in her heart.

He lifted a hand and let his fingers graze the side of her face. "Amen."

She released a deep sigh. Then she realized that others expected her to be checking patients. "We'd best go before we are missed."

He nodded and held the door open for her. "Can I see you tonight?"

She paused. It wouldn't be easy to process his leaving, but she did want to take advantage of what time they had together. So, she nodded before moving farther into the recovery area and forced herself to focus on her work and not on Dr. Hendry.

Which, with lips still tingling from his kiss, proved to be a tremendous undertaking.

Theodore stood amidst the buildings and waited. Would Rose come to see him one more time? He wished more than anything that she could see him depart, but that wouldn't be wise. Not with the emotions between them. And certainly not while keeping the appearance of a strictly professional relationship. Not that he believed anyone thought that's all it was.

He had seen the looks shot his way by other nurses and Dr. Donovan. They all knew. And it didn't bother him one bit. He cared a great deal for Rose. Now that the danger was over in this plague, he would focus on wooing her. Not that she had ever shied away from his affections.

Glancing at his watch, his stomach did a flip. Would he have to leave without seeing her one more time? That brought a pang. He would wait. He just had to give her a proper farewell.

The sun gave a slight peek over the horizon. His time was becoming short. Had something happened to her? Fear rushed through him.

Then a crunch of grass drew his attention toward the barracks. There she was. He breathed out his deep relief.

She stumbled a bit, and the fear immediately returned. What if the flu wasn't on the decline? What if she had contracted it?

Not caring who was watching, he crossed the yard to where she was, gripping at her arms.

"Rose?" he breathed the word. Nothing else would come.

Her eyes widened. At his tone? Or because she felt ill?

"What's the matter?" He managed to press out.

"I..." She set a hand to her forehead. "I'm just fighting some allergies." She sniffled as if to reinforce her plight.

"Are you sure?" His tone was still rather desperate. And he hated that. But so many Spanish flu patients initially presented with hay-fever-type symptoms. How could she be certain that was all?

"Yes." She wiped at her nose with a handkerchief.

He wasn't confident about her self-diagnosis. Yet he wasn't certain him pushing would be well-received. Though he couldn't not question it. "Other than congestion—"

She waved him off. "There is no need to fret. Really. I have all the classic symptoms: congestion, sinus pressure, my ears even feel a little clogged."

He supposed she was right. There was not really a reason for him to fear as long as her symptoms remained mild. But he couldn't completely dispel the anxiety within. "Perhaps I should push to stay. Maybe this is a resurgence of the—"

"You know as well as I do that you can't ignore a direct order. And there is no reason to think this is anything but a little hay fever. Happens every year when the rains stir everything up."

He nodded. It made sense. "I should at least see you back to your barracks." Turning in that direction, he started to lead her that way.

"No." She put a hand to his arm. "I came to see you off. Albeit a bit late."

No doubt due to fighting these symptoms. "But you stumbled."

She gave him a hard look. "Don't go babying me." Her words were harsh. "My ears are clogged. I just...lost my balance for a second. Honestly, would you worry so much about a patient who presented this way?"

He shoved a hand through his hair and thought about his next words. Though they came without censure. "But you're not another patient. You're you."

She blinked. Almost as if disbelieving.

Had the love notes he had left her since the shift in their relationship not iterated how much he cared? He did often have to pull himself back from expressing the full force of the emotions. Perhaps to the point the letters had become a bit more...sterile.

"I know you care," she whispered. Had she heard his thoughts? Or read his heart? "And I think you know how I..." She looked down. As if she feared voicing her own heart's leaning.

"Rose..." The word fell tenderly from his lips. He loved the feel of it coming off his tongue. "I do care. So very much. In fact, I—"

She pressed fingers to his mouth. "Don't."

What could she mean? Did she not feel the same for him? Is that why she stopped him?

"I don't want you to say things that can't be unsaid. Those words mean too much to say them in a moment and regret them in another."

He lifted both hands to frame her face. "I won't."

Her breath caught and her lips parted.

He wanted to fight the urge to press them with his, but what was the use? He felt it. He needed their interactions of the last weeks to end on this note. "I know what I feel. And there's no other way to explain it away. I love you."

She took in a sharp gasp.

Then he covered her lips with his own.

The kiss held promises for the future. Promises he intended to keep.

When they parted, he rested his forehead to hers. "Write me?"

"Every day," came her breathy response.

He wanted to stay in that moment forever. But the tires crunching on the dirt-packed path drew him from the moment. He started to disentangle himself.

She allowed it, pressing the handkerchief to her nose and blotting her eyes as well.

He picked up his pack and then caressed her cheek once more, memorizing her features.

Then he turned and forced his feet to carry him opposite.

"Theodore," she called out.

He halted, shifting to look over his shoulder.

She took a couple of ragged breaths. "I love you, too."

The words penetrated to his heart. It was all he could do not to rush back to her, wrap her in his arms, and kiss her with all the passion he felt.

But it was better this way.

He tipped his hat to her and offered her a small salute. "I'll be waiting for that first letter."

She smiled. "You can plan on it."

Then he made his legs turn him back toward the transport and lengthen the distance between them. Even as it tore at his heart, the knowledge that she loved him was a balm, and he held it close long after the jeep carried him away.

## ELEVEN

# surviving

*April 24, 2020*
*Trammel Apartments*
*Cordova, TN*

S cott leaned forward at the dining table, setting the most recently read of his great grandparents' letters to the side. He wondered if his mother realized what all they contained. It was a sweet story—a love sparked during a horrible pandemic. Well, the beginning of what would become a pandemic.

It seemed Theodore suspected that it would rise to that level all along, but that may not be the case...somewhat like the coronavirus pandemic. Some may have thought it might gain such global traction, but most were oblivious in the months before it happened. In his case, he only hoped that *his* love story would survive it.

He pushed that thought to the side and focused on something that had been nagging at him...the issue of the aspirin. It seemed odd that this Dr. Donovan would prescribe more than the average over the counter dose. He did a quick internet search on his phone.

Aspirin was indeed used to treat many of the patients suffering from the Spanish flu. It was the only thing even remotely effective for symptoms. But many doctors unknowingly overdosed their patients. That tended to cause...oh my, the same thing Rose had noticed in her patient. Agitation, fever, wheezing, convulsions, confusion, and...coma. So, Rose had been right all along. Her concern about the dosing was founded. If only he could reach back in time and tell her.

He continued scanning the online article. For many of the patients overdosed on aspirin, their lungs filled with fluid. One of the same outcomes caused by the Spanish flu. Wow. That would have made isolating the problem very difficult.

Realizing that his knowledge of the 1918 pandemic was spotty at best, he kept reading. Each bit of information gleaned caused the tightness in his chest to hurt more. One third of the world's population was infected. And ten percent of those infected would die. More lost to the Spanish flu than World War I. That couldn't be possible. How had he not heard about this before?

But he remembered...Theodore's letter detailed how the military wanted to suppress any news about it to prevent panic. This article iterated that as well. Most governments censored the information to keep anything negative from the public. They wanted everyone on board the war effort.

So different from the COVID pandemic. If anything, they were over communicating. To the point that not everything could be true.

Scott frowned. In fact, most of the news sources he found to be biased and unreliable. And he questioned everything they put out. If only Brianne had a little more of that skepticism. Everything made her more afraid.

And...unlike the aspirin being pushed on patients in 1918, the few medications recommended for treating COVID were being rejected. Perhaps for good reason. All the more felt after reading about the aspirin being overused.

He scanned farther, wondering what brought the Spanish flu pandemic to an end. Did they find a cure? As he read on, he frowned. There was no cure. There wasn't even good information discovered until thirty years later when better research equipment and methods came around. Would the same be true of the COVID pandemic? Would there be no cure? No hope for the thousands who were sick and dying?

Paul walked out of his room just then. "You up already?" The guy was still in his pajamas. He'd been sleeping in more than usual.

"It's ten thirty." Scott kept his response level and plain, devoid of accusation or judgment.

While he hated to see how his friend had become so listless of late, he knew it was unlike Paul. In the beginning, Paul had embraced the extra time to work on his music. But over the course of the last few weeks, he'd been sleeping more, not showering, and getting lost in TV shows. No more work on his art. In fact, he seemed to have been zapped of all motivation to do so.

"There's a fresh pot of coffee," Scott said as he jerked his head toward the kitchen. "I needed a little boost myself."

"Thanks." Paul trudged to the counter and poured himself a cup. "What does your day look like?" His words came on a yawn.

"I'm hoping to FaceTime with Brianne later. But I have some work stuff to do first."

"You finally going to tell her about the wedding venue?" Paul offered a meaningful glance in Scott's direction.

"I will, I will...I just..." He didn't know how to finish.

"I know. You were ready to tell her then the governor's most recent announcement came." Paul took a sip from his mug as he moved toward the couch.

"Well, you remember how she took that."

"I can't imagine why she wouldn't be thrilled the governor will let the shelter at home order expire at the end of the month. It's the best news I've heard since that order was issued," Paul groused.

His general demeanor had been pulled down as well. No longer the happy-go-lucky friend who saw the best in everyone. Now his whole mood seemed dim.

"She's still afraid of getting COVID. And opening up everything, she feels, will increase the spread."

"It might. But we can't go on living like this. I'd rather take my chances with the virus."

Scott nodded. He felt much the same. But he also understood the caution and the measures taken. Mostly because he lived this with Brianne and her trepidations tempering his general thoughts about the pandemic. "Just be gentle with Brie if you talk to her. She's at a vulnerable place."

Paul nodded. "Sure." But then he turned on the TV. "Is this going to bother you?"

That was kind. The last several days, Paul had seemed to not care about that. As if he forgot that Scott still had to work.

"No. I was going to head into my room to get back to coding."

"Okay." This time, Paul didn't bother looking over.

Scott gathered his coffee, the letters, and his phone before stepping toward his room.

He settled into his desk chair and set the things in his arms down. His gaze caught on the engagement picture of him and Brie. She was smiling. A grin so brilliant and happy it was like the sunshine. And there was a light in her eyes he hadn't seen in months. He frowned and closed his eyes.

*Lord, help her see You in this pandemic. Your hand guiding us and sustaining us. Help her find the joy of her salvation and the joy of knowing You again.*

Though the prayer was quick and simple, it was heartfelt. And he trusted that the Holy Spirit would continue to intercede on his behalf and on Brianne's. He hoped that God would show him when to push and when to listen to Brianne. Absent of judgment. Absent of what *he* thought was best.

Brianne needed to find her way to trusting God on her own. He could help her, but he couldn't force it. Nor did he want to.

The sound from the TV seeped into Scott's room. Why did Paul have to listen to it so loudly? But Scott just reached for his ear buds and dialed up his favorite playlist.

Then he turned his attention back to the JavaScript on his screen. He would have to hack through this sooner or later. Why not now? At least it might take his mind off these troubling things.

Just as he started to get into a groove, his phone pinged. Who could that be?

It was Brianne's contact that popped across the screen with a text.

Did you know about this!?!

A lump formed in his throat. Had she somehow found out about Cherry Lane Inn? How? He braced himself for her possible reaction and clicked on the message and corresponding link.

*April 24, 2020*
*Wyngate Apartments*
*Cordova, TN*

Brianne held her breath as she waited for Scott's text response. How could he not tell her about the toilet paper shortage? She would have been stocking up by now. How could she have missed it? There were graphics all over social media...something she had been avoiding...but the signs were all there.

His reply finally came through.

FaceTime?

She rolled her eyes. That was the last thing she wanted. But if she told him that, he'd have...thoughts...about that. And probably silent judgments about her stability. What a rocky path she walked...

Okay. Give me a minute.

A minute for what? To adjust her appearance? Become less agitated?

One of the places on her arm started to bleed. Oh goodness...she had told Sheri she would try to curb the picking by keeping her hands busy. How long had she been picking at them?

She sighed. It was useless. All of it.

Might as well FaceTime as she was. Scott either accepted her with all her challenges or not. Now was the time to find out. Not two years into a bumpy marriage.

She clenched her teeth and forced herself to hit the FaceTime button. But as she did so, she cancelled it out.

Can we Zoom instead?

That was an odd request. But she wanted to honor her words to Sheri and grab her crochet project. She couldn't hold the phone and work the yarn. But if they were on Zoom, she could set up her laptop on the desk.

> Okay. Do you still have the link for my personal Zoom room?

His response had been slow in coming, but he agreed. With any luck, he wouldn't ask her about it once they were chatting.

> Yes. Hopping on now.

She grabbed the basket with her yarn and crochet hooks and stepped to her desk. It took little effort to open the computer and find his link in her emails.

The window signaling to her that the host would let her in came up. And a moment later, Scott's face was on the screen.

"Hey!" He seemed unsure of himself somehow. Why it appeared that way wasn't clear to her, but it was there all the same.

"Hey," she said, keeping her words subdued. Again, she wasn't sure why she did that. But she picked up her latest crochet project and worked the yarn and hook. It gave her something other than his face to focus on. And that calmed her.

"I wasn't able to pull up the link you sent. I think it may be redirecting me."

"Oh." She glanced at the screen. "It was an article about the toilet paper shortage. Is that true? Has there been a problem with that?"

He let out a long breath. Was he relieved? "Yes. It's been a big problem all over the country."

"Why is there a run on toilet paper?" Her frustration no doubt seeped into her tone. But it didn't make sense.

"Apparently people started stockpiling it. Then it became harder to find. And now that the shelter at home has gone on longer than expected, the manufacturers are allegedly having a difficult time keeping up with demand. A lot of these people are not usually home so much. And the office-style products are the only thing available."

"I...um...have that on my grocery list this week."

He frowned. "You need me to go to the grocery store for you?"

"Yeah." His confusion surprised her. "If that's okay."

"It's fine. But the shelter at home order has been lifted."

Was he expecting her to go then? She swallowed then pressed into the moment despite her trepidation. "I...don't know that I feel safe enough."

"Oh." His features remained quizzical. As if he still didn't understand. "I'll grab your things then."

She nodded and refocused on her work.

"What are you doing there?" His lips curled at the ends, but it was obviously forced.

"I'm crocheting. Trying to get this blanket done." Why couldn't she just tell him? Let him judge if he wanted. But there was reason to be honest. Though, as she roused the courage, he spoke.

"I haven't seen you work on that in a while."

"Yeah. Well, I wanted to get it done before I think about changing the colors in my bedroom."

He let out a light laugh. The throaty chuckle of his was always endearing.

"Listen," he broke in again. "I need to chat with you about something."

He sounded serious. She jerked her regard to the screen. Could she handle it if he questioned her unease with going out yet? What if he suggested she let her psychiatrist know? That wasn't necessary, surely. She had just in the last couple of months started feeling good about her meds.

"What's up?" Her attempt to keep it casual probably showed.

"I wish I could talk to you about it in person, though. This feels so...distant."

Did it? This was the only contact she'd had with anyone in the last month. It felt stifled, yes, but normal.

"I don't know..." She let the sentence trail. How could she express to him just how nervous that made her? How could he not understand by now?

"Could we do a car date?"

"A what?" If she didn't want to get groceries from him directly at the door, how was she going to sit in a car with him? A flush filled her. As did the urge to pick at her arms, play with her hair... anything but face him.

"We would meet in a parking lot with our driver's sides facing each other. A parking spot between us."

She let out a breath. She hadn't been outside since the end of March. But this was a lot less intimidating than climbing into the passenger seat of his car.

"Maybe we could go to a coffee shop. The one on Poplar with the drive thru."

If he wanted to grab coffee for himself before they met, she could understand. But she doubted she'd feel safe interacting with the barista...even if it was through a no-contact window.

"I think that might work."

"You don't sound so sure. Look, if you'd rather—"

"No," she interjected. "I'd like to give it a try." She couldn't very well stay in this apartment forever. This may be a doable step in her readjustment to normal...or whatever new normal would look like for her and for the people of the world.

He grinned. "Great. What about this afternoon?"

She sucked in a breath. That was soon.

"I think it would be good for y—" He paused, then continued, "For us."

She knew what he almost said. *Good for you.* As if she were the only one stressed about all the changes. Maybe she wasn't ready for this.

"Okay. If you're not ready...perhaps we can go tomorrow?"

That was still intimidating. But she pushed down her rising trepidation. "Okay. How does mid-morning sound?"

Why had she said that? Mid-morning? That was in the first part of the day. It would, she reminded herself, prevent her from stressing about it all day. Yes, that was best.

"Sure." His eyes lit up as if that was the best news in weeks. Was it? Was he so desperate to see her in person?

She forced a smile onto her features that was likely obviously faked.

"Listen..." He leaned forward. "I'd like to stay on longer, but I have work to do for a release and a meeting with my manager in an hour. I'd like to have more to report on my progress by then."

She nodded. "Understood. I'll send you my grocery list."

"I'll try to text or FaceTime tonight."

Jerking her head in assent, she wiggled closer to the monitor screen. "Hey..."

"Yeah?" His bright eyes were so easy to look at...full of hope and promise.

"I miss you. And I am looking forward to seeing you tomorrow."

He let out a breath and his shoulders relaxed. "Me too, Brie. I miss you so much."

That did warm her heart, heating her from within. "Tomorrow, then." She held up a hand in a wave as she maneuvered her fingers over the trackpad. The cursor hovered over the button to end the call and video feed. Clicking it, she watched Scott's face disappear.

And tried not to think on the car date. Or the possibility of bringing the coronavirus back to her apartment.

She tried. And failed.

*April 25, 2020*
*The Java Cup*
*Memphis, TN*

Scott eased off Poplar Avenue and into the coffee shop's drive thru line. He scanned the parking lot for Brianne's car but came up empty. In his eagerness to see her, he had gotten here a bit early. He glanced at his car's clock. Okay, a lot early.

But he would do it again. He was going to see Brianne today. In person. For the first time in nearly a month. It seemed too good to be true.

Was it? Would she shy away from their intended meeting?

He prayed not. It would be good for her, right? If not because she missed him—though he hoped she did—but good for her to get out and about.

The car behind him honked. Shaking his thoughts clear, he realized the one in front of him had moved. How long ago, he didn't know. Perhaps the person behind him was being impatient, or maybe not. Either way, he'd sat here for long enough to need a nudge.

He lifted his hand to wave an apology to the driver behind. Looking in his rearview mirror, he got a corresponding wave from the dark-haired woman.

Moving his car forward, he then placed his order. He was tempted to order Brianne's caramel latte but thought twice. She probably wouldn't let him give it to her out of his car. So, he told the barista that was all before driving around. When he turned the corner, he saw that the way to the window was clear. How long had he been sitting there? His face heated. Oh, well.

He paid and collected his drink from a tray the barista held out the window. The thought occurred to him that it was a little senseless...the barista had to touch the drink to put it on the tray. Then he got it. This protected the staff inside from him. For as he lifted the drink from the tray, he did not have contact with the barista or the tray. Still a somewhat unnecessary worry, but he tried to understand the reasoning.

As he maneuvered his car to the parking lot, he spotted Brianne's Corolla as far away from the building as she could get. Such that she was against the edge of the parking lot. He had to back into the spot to be somewhat facing her driver's side with his.

He had not rolled his window up yet, so he left it and leaned slightly out to see her better.

She waved from inside the car then put on a mask and rolled her window down.

It was a bit of a punch to the gut, but, again, he wanted to understand. Even if he didn't.

"Hey," she said, offering a little wave.

And he let himself relax. All of this was probably hard for her. He needed to give her credit for the effort.

"You are a wonderful sight," he said, and marveled at how her hair had grown. In most of their video chats, she'd had her hair pulled back into a ponytail. Now, it fell around her shoulders in curls. Curls he wanted to reach out and touch. He turned his attention to her face and drank in her features, what of them he could see.

My goodness, he missed her.

Only then did he note the misting in her eyes. She looked as if she might cry. Was she so moved?

That made him choke a bit against the lump forming in his throat.

She swiped at her eyes. "I have missed you."

"I know." He smiled, hoping he could encourage her and distract himself from tearing up at the same time.

As he shifted in his seat, a breeze blew past her car and toward him. The smell of sanitizer and bleach wafted over him. It was strong. Had she worked to clean her car earlier? Perhaps that was the only way she could have come...to have her car germ free. Or as germ free as she could make it.

There was no way to completely clear the air of germs. And maybe that's what made her uneasy. For as much as she seemed pleased, she also appeared shaky.

"What have you been up to today?" Her question was a safe one. But he wanted to get what he needed to out and over with.

Would she be more upset about the venue cancelling? Or about him hiding it from her for these weeks?

He shrugged. "I've had a chat with Jack about one of the ongoing projects at work. Nothing much else."

She nodded. "What about Paul? How is he?"

Should he tell the truth or instead ease her mind? He opted for the truth. "He's been better. Struggling to motivate himself these days."

"Yeah?" Her eyes drooped at the corners as if she frowned.

"Yeah. At first, he got a ton accomplished...with all that free time. But now, he is more content to just veg. Most days he doesn't even get out of his pajamas."

"Huh." Her thoughts seemed to drift. Had he misspoken? Was she in the same situation? He thought back and couldn't recall seeing much of what she wore in their FaceTime calls. He'd really only homed in on her face.

"But I'm sure he'll be back to himself soon. Now that the order is lifted."

She looked down at her hands, still on the steering wheel. As if she could take off at any moment.

He swallowed. He hadn't wanted to make her leery of him or of this time. "Hey, I found some toilet paper!"

She raised her eyebrows. "You did?"

"I happened upon the Dollar General just as the restocking truck was there. Sure enough, they had just delivered some."

She let out a sigh. "Thank goodness."

Silence fell between them. It was awkward. Maybe it was best to get out what he came to say. Then let things fall where they may.

"Hey, I need to tell you something."

She jerked back toward him. "Yeah. You mentioned that. What's going on?" Her eyes reflected a level of anxiety he had not expected. What did she think he would say?

"Cherry Lane Inn called and said they have to cancel our wedding date."

Brianne's eyes widened. Because it just occurred to her that they still had something like that in the plans? Had she forgotten about their wedding? "Oh...I see."

"The lady who met with us, Rochelle, called and said they could rebook when things are more settled and clearer. And if we wanted to just cancel, we may not get our deposit back."

Brianne's mouth became a thin line, and her expressive eyes dulled.

"Are you okay?" The question came out before he could stop it.

"Yeah."

It took him a second. Did she mean she was okay about the news? Or okay in general?

"We don't have to talk about it now. I told her I'd let her know in a few weeks. So, she isn't expecting a call until at least next week."

"Wait a second. When did she call?" Brianne's gaze pierced him.

Uh oh. He had said too much. He pushed out a breath. "Sometime around April seventeenth."

"Scott, that was more than a week ago. Why are you just now telling me?" There was a hardness to her voice that he knew he deserved.

"I...didn't want to upset you. You've had such a hard time with everything. And then the shelter at home order lifted...and you struggled then, too. Besides—"

"So you thought you needed to decide what I could and could not handle?" The hard edge became sharp.

He blew out air. "It's not like that." Except it was. He had wanted to protect her. And in doing so had made choices about what she could manage emotionally. "I'm sorry, Brie. I really am. I shouldn't have done that."

She looked ahead, out her windshield, hands gripping her steering wheel.

"But you've been a bit...moody lately. I just wanted—"

"You wanted to protect me; I get that. But maybe I don't need you to." She turned a fiery gaze on him.

And he wondered...was she really upset? Or was this the product of one more thing piled onto her overloaded shoulders?

"I...need to go." She reached for her seatbelt.

"Brie, don't. Look, I'm sorry."

"I heard you the first time."

"Please don't go."

She paused but turned to him then. "This has just been too much on me today. Getting out, coming here, this news."

He didn't miss the irony that she was angry and that had brought his fears to fruition. She wasn't handling the news well. It had not been up to him. Yet he had made it his decision.

She started rolling up her window.

"Please, wait a second," he called out.

The window stopped its upward climb, but she didn't look his way again.

"I love you. And I'm so very sorry. I wish you didn't have to go. I've missed you so, so much." He could hear the wavering of his own voice. And he hated that weakness.

"I love you, too." Her words were flat. "And I accept your apology."

He breathed easier.

"But...I still...I just have to go."

She rolled the window up the rest of the way. And he was helpless to watch as the woman he planned to pledge his life to pulled away.

# *distance*

August 23, 1918
Fort Campbell
Clarksville, TN

Theodore,

I cannot express how much I miss you. It's been too long. The cases of Spanish flu continue to increase here. I suppose it wasn't all over in the Spring as we had believed (and hoped). I pray you are finding answers. We need them badly...

Theodore set her letter to the side. The desperation in her words cut at him. He wished, too, that he had answers. But all the research on the underlying bacterium had come to naught. It gave him pause to wonder if it wasn't something else...something more nefarious than *Haemophilus influenzae.* In truth, it must be. For nothing they did to learn about it and fight it brought about the desired results.

This second wave of the Spanish flu had the makings of a true worldwide pandemic. He wished to heaven that his superiors would listen. But even if they could stop the movement of soldiers around the globe, how would that impact the war and the fate of millions?

But troops being shipped here and there all over the world, interacting with many at major ports and in the close quarters of trenches...it would only aid the spread of this horrid illness. And probably had.

Still, the sickness was not as major a concern for the powers that be as was this war. And he could understand that. What would they gain if they tamped down this flu only to lose what had been thus far gained on the war front?

It was truly difficult. And as much as he disagreed with the suppression of information, he was rather glad he didn't have to weigh that decision.

That didn't help Rose or the others at Fort Riley. Dr. Donovan and the rest of the medical staff were no doubt being pushed to their breaking point. How he wished his commanding officer would send him back, but they deemed his research of top priority.

This frustrated him. But if he were to make a major break-through in treatment, it would make all the difference. Though no matter how many late nights and early mornings he managed, no answers were forthcoming. It was almost as if he were on the wrong trajectory.

The flu continued to disproportionately afflict young adults. It made no sense. Unless, it was their strong immune system that played a part in the illness response. Any and all efforts to control symptoms had been for naught. He even wondered if the aspirin regimen was of any use.

Did they have anything else to fight it? The whole situation was grim. The numbers coming in of those infected and dying had only increased. This was larger scale than it had been in the Spring. And far more deadly.

A knock on his door drew his attention.

"Yes?"

The door opened a crack. It was his assistant. A fine medical mind, but only recently graduated. He was curious and eager. Not that either of those things had made any difference in their efforts.

"Dr. Hendry, I have those results from the recent culture."

As much as all other research led to dead ends, Theodore was still hopeful. They needed a break. And soon. "Yes?"

The younger man shook his head.

Theodore frowned and made a conscious effort to keep his shoulders from drooping. What now? What might they try next?

"If I may." The younger man stepped into the office as he spoke. "I have noticed that most patients are suffering from what seems a secondary infection of the lungs."

Theodore nodded and resisted the urge to rub a hand down his face.

"Might we look further into that? Or even follow up with the survivors? I suspect there are lingering effects of this drastic illness."

Again, Theodore nodded, slowly, as he considered the man's words. Their focus had been on the primary illness. If there was a secondary infection that they could treat, would that save lives?

And if it were possible to isolate whatever had allowed the survivors to escape death, there may be answers there.

"Do the interviews. Reach out to Dr. Lance Donovan at Fort Riley. They saw a large number of cases in the first go around. They could perhaps question those that pulled through."

The younger man nodded and shifted toward the door.

"Good thoughts," Theodore called after him. "I'll be in the lab soon."

The man beamed at the compliment and slipped out of the office.

Theodore leaned back in his chair and looked at the picture of Rose he kept on his desk. He had insisted she send him a photograph a month ago. It calmed him somehow to be able to look on her features. There was also that inner push, that desire to fix this for her. For as long as this illness afflicted the military camps, the greater the risk to her.

He would beat this. He had to.

Rose swiped at the soap as she washed her hands. The scrubbing had become more a part of her routine. Before patients, between patients, after finishing. She wanted to pull down the mask that covered the lower portion of her face, but she dare not while in the sick ward. The risk was too great.

There was little the medical personnel could do to prevent their own illness...besides the mask and hand washing. And she would do so diligently.

She finished and moved out of the ward. Should she try the mess hall and grab some much needed nourishment? Or did her bunk call to her too loudly to be ignored? She was weary. So weary.

The cot it was then. She trudged toward the barracks with defeat weighing on her shoulders. One would think a nurse would become numbed to the loss. Especially after all the dying she'd encountered over the last year. But she wasn't.

Nor did she want to be. Every death mattered. They were lives snuffed out. Needlessly.

And nothing she did was making a difference. Except perhaps

that she would sit with them when they were in pain, comfort them when they were afraid, and be a kind presence when they needed one.

But it was exhausting—physically, mentally, and emotionally. When would it be enough?

She had feared her allergies last Spring might be the beginning of a flu for her, but it had just been that—hay fever. Thank goodness. She had not wanted to entertain what it would mean for her to contract the Spanish flu. Her harsh words to Theodore had been self-preserving and not very thoughtful. Had she ever apologized for that?

Speaking with him through letters only was difficult. She wasn't much for expressing herself in writing. But she was growing that skill. He was so eloquent and always seemed to know what to say.

Not her. She struggled with the practice. Always had.

Her thoughts drifted to her family in Illinois. She needed to send some more money this month if possible. National rationing had made things all the more difficult for the large family. And the United States government pushing all production toward the war effort left the civilians in a bit of a lurch.

Yes, she would send as much as she could spare. Her living expenses were few.

She stepped into the barracks and headed toward her cot then all but collapsed on the thin mattress. The thought occurred to her that she should change her clothes or maybe get under the blanket. But she did neither. There was little energy to do more than shift onto her pillow.

But her swirling thoughts kept her mind active. How could she shut those down? The faces of her current patients and even past patients filled her unseeing closed eyes. Without reprieve.

*Lord, I beseech You. Give me rest.*

Then the images quieted. All but one—Walter.

He had been kind. And good. But he had been more a friend than anything else. Had she cared for him romantically? She had believed it was so...or could be so.

Until she met Theodore. The feelings he elicited in her were nearly overwhelming. The emotions mixed and twirled together until they were difficult to separate—the passion she felt, the hunger for his presence, the draw to him. Yet she often wondered if there were deeper things between them than surface attraction.

The more she shared herself, the more he accepted her as she was, the more she believed it was possible.

Still, she hadn't wanted to share about her family. What would he think? He had come from a more affluent background. Had he ever known want?

She had reason to doubt that.

Pushing that to the side, she opted to dwell on the pleasant feelings that warmed her core when she thought of him. And his words to her.

Her mind calmed and drifted toward sweet slumber.

Until the door to the barracks slammed open.

She startled upright. "What's the matter?" Had something happened? Perhaps one of her patients had...

It was the younger nurse that kept the cot to her right. "My apologies, Rose. I didn't realize anyone was in here. When I didn't see you in the mess hall, I thought for sure you still lingered with your patients."

Rose nodded and lay back down. "I was too tired."

"Oh, never mind me then. You just go right ahead and...wait."

Rose opened an eye.

The woman reached into her pocket. "I did grab a letter for you at mail call."

Rose leaned up, propping her torso onto her bent arm. "For me?"

Her first thought was of Theodore. But she had received a

letter from him yesterday. Had he found a need to send one right after? Maybe one of his experiments showed something promising...

The girl extracted the letter and handed it to Rose.

A glance at the front proved it was not, in fact, from Theodore, but from her mother.

She sighed. Not that she didn't wish for word from home. But she craved news from Theodore. On many levels.

Lying on her back, she tore at the envelope's seal and slid the paper out. Glancing over the letter, she drank in her mother's words. But something caught her attention farther down. A sickness had overtaken the town. And their family.

Rose sat up and gasped. The Spanish flu had found her family.

And she was hundreds of miles away. Helpless.

## THIRTEEN

# *working on it*

*April 28, 2020*
*Wyngate Apartments*
*Cordova, TN*

Brianne parked in her spot. Thank goodness, she had arrived. It was getting difficult to see straight through her anger. How could Scott do that? He just decided she couldn't handle it and then buried it? Did he not trust her at all?

Except...

Something in the back of her mind pled with her to listen, but she refused.

Grabbing the sanitizer from her purse, she poured some on her hands then put her mask back on. This had been a mistake. Going out. Trying to be somewhat in the normal world with the real people. A mistake.

She opened her door, careful not to hit the car next to her. And she slid out, again, trying to not even come close to making contact with her neighbor's car. Who knew what germs that guy was coming in contact with? She certainly had no idea.

The walk to her apartment door was brief as she had quickened her stride. What if she were to come across one of the other tenants of the building? Was it now considered rude to keep walking and give them wide berth? Either way, she would have to risk being rude.

Now at her door, she re-sanitized and slid the antiseptic on her doorknob then opened it and rushed into the safer interior. But she stopped. How could she risk bringing these possibly germy clothes into her safe home? So, she pulled off her pants and t-shirt, discarding them before sanitizing her hands again. She left her clothes there by the door and went to grab a robe. A shower would be in order after she got these clothes in the laundry.

After pushing hands through the robe's sleeves, she reached for her latex gloves and made short work of getting the contaminated clothing into the wash.

As she closed the lid, she heard a loud knock on the door. A knock?

She wasn't dressed to entertain anyone...not that she would be letting anyone in. Who could it be anyway? She wasn't in the mood.

"Yes?" she called as she stepped toward the door, still sure to keep her space from it.

"Brie, it's me. I'm sorry...but I couldn't leave things like that." Scott. He had followed her home?

No, he had come here looking for her. He couldn't have followed her if she'd had those minutes to get in and start the laundry. How long had he lingered, trying to decide what to do?

It didn't matter.

"I don't know that this is the right time," she hollered.

"Please, Brie, talk to me."

A thump on the other side of the door had her wondering if he set his forehead there, or his hands, or maybe even leaned his whole body there? Had he no thought to the possibility of what was on that door?

"Scott, I...I'm just angry right now. I'll calm down. Then we can talk. Maybe FaceTime later?"

"I'm not asking you to let me in, but I just...need to talk to you."

She weighed her options. Perhaps she could insist he leave. She could walk into her bedroom and close the door so she couldn't hear him anymore. Or...she could prioritize reconciliation with him over her desire to be right. He wasn't even saying she wasn't right.

"I love you. And I don't want to fight. I made a bone-headed mistake. And I'm sorry."

His words swayed her in light of her consideration. He had admitted his guilt. And apologized. But her anger flared still. She couldn't quite quell it.

"I just...I want us to be okay." Came his words.

She did want that too, didn't she? It didn't feel like that right now.

"I treated you horribly. I should have told you right after that call from the venue."

"Yes, you should have." There was an edge to her voice.

"I know. And I'm hoping...praying...you can forgive me." His words spilled out, a desperate cry from his wounded heart. Or was it?

But what did the Bible say about forgiveness? God forgave her, so she needed to extend forgiveness. Not that the wrong doesn't exist, but she is handing the hurt and anger over to God.

That was easier said than done.

"I just want you to think I'm capable. And stronger than this."

"I do. I can totally see where my actions didn't speak that way. But I do. I just...worry about you."

She knew that was true. And she loved that about him. The

way he put her first. The way he always looked for ways to serve her.

Her hand fell against the cool surface of the door. Had she stepped closer? The urge to pull her hand back was nearly over-whelming. But she maintained that contact, wishing she could reach to him through the door, though warily glad that she couldn't.

"I do love you," she said on a sigh. "And I forgive you."

"Thank you." His voice was quiet but firm. Contrite.

"But I need you to understand what this is like for me." She needed that more than anything in that moment. Someone who wasn't questioning her or judging her...just supporting her. No matter how it might seem.

"I am trying." That was honest at least. "I do want to under-stand. But...I just don't...most of the time."

She held her breath, waiting for the rest.

"I can't go through this pandemic without trusting God. And... sweetheart, it seems you trust your ability to control everything more."

Ouch. That hurt. Her ire fired in her stomach, and she opened her mouth, but he continued.

"I want to understand, I do. But I want you to understand me, too."

Another prickle to her heart. Was that true? Was she not extending the same courtesy *to him* that she wanted *from him*?

An unpleasant feeling settled in her midsection, pressing the anger down. He wasn't wrong. And that hurt.

"Listen, Scott, I..." She held up her hand and let it fall back to her side. "You're right. I haven't spent much time trying to under-stand where you're coming from."

He let out a shaky breath. One she was surprised to hear through the door.

"But I don't know that you know what it's like on this side.

I'm scared of everything and everyone. The coronavirus germs could be anywhere...on a gas pump handle, on the outside of my car from someone brushing against it...even in the breeze blowing by me. It's terrifying. And I'm almost paralyzed with worry that someone I know will get sick and even..." She couldn't say it. Couldn't put words to that.

"I know. I worry about that, too."

He did? "How come you aren't so fearful?"

"How many times does the Bible tell us not to be anxious but to trust in Him?"

"Isn't there a place to trust and be smart about risk?"

"There is." He sounded less sure about that.

Could they be looking at two sides of the same coin? Or did she lack trust in God to be in charge?

For trust in Him didn't mean she or someone she loved wouldn't get sick. There was never a promise of that. And *that* was more difficult to swallow than anything else. Even if she trusted, it didn't guarantee the outcome she wanted. She leaned her back against the door and slid to a sitting position.

"Brie?" He sounded concerned. Had he heard her settling against the door?

"I'm here."

"I thought...you just got really quiet."

"I was thinking." She caught herself picking at her arm and forced her hands to play with the fabric at the hem of the robe instead.

"I want to hold you."

"I know." This time there wasn't fear that he would push, just a sadness. Because, she wanted that too but was unable to give him—or herself—that comfort.

"I also worry about you being alone in there all the time."

She nodded. If she were honest, she was becoming more concerned herself.

"Would you consider going to your parents' house? Or to Latasha's?"

The trepidation rising in her gut was difficult to push down. But she said, "I will think about it. I promise."

She heard something slide on the outside of the door. And she imagined him sitting just as she was, propped up against the outside of the door.

"That's all I ask."

She nodded but knew he couldn't see that. Though the lump in her throat made it difficult to speak.

"Oh...and one more thing."

Her brows lowered. He was going to ask one more thing? Would he, then, push to be let in? With his words having chipped at the barrier around her heart, did she have the strength to deny him? "Yes?"

"Pray with me?"

The remaining barrier erected by her anger shattered, and it took several moments before she could compose herself enough to speak. "Yes."

Then he started praying. And she relaxed into his words, beseeching God to be with them and be their rock.

Lord knew she needed Him to be. More now than ever.

*April 30, 2020*
*Trammel Apartments*
*Cordova, TN*

Scott opened his eyes. The world looked a bit blurry without his contacts. But he reached to his nightstand and grabbed his glasses. Then things cleared up.

He sat up in his bed, leaning against the headboard, and tried to settle into being awake. It was not easy as his dreams had been pervasive. In his sleep, he had lived Brianne getting COVID. It was awful. Probably the product of their conversation yesterday and their prayer time. The enemy would take any and every opportunity to make him worry and doubt God's goodness.

So, he prayed. *Lord, help me to trust You. Especially when it's difficult. Help me trust You with Brianne, the most precious gift You've given me. Well, aside from salvation, of course. Keep her and comfort her.*

She would be leaving for her folks' house today. It had been a long time coming and he was proud of her. This was a humungous step for her. One he did not take lightly.

It stung to think that she would be so far away. But it was more important she be mentally and emotionally well than close enough to do more car dates.

He spotted the place on his desk where the letters had sat. Yesterday, he had taken them to Brianne. There was just this feeling about them that they may offer her hope and a different perspective on the pandemic. One that he prayed God would work into the reading. There were some good things in the conversation, as it were, between his great grandparents.

The urge to FaceTime her was pressing, but he set that to the side. He was an early riser and Brie...well, she was more of a night owl. There was little desire to face her anger at being awakened before ten.

Turning his smart watch upward, the time displayed on the screen. Eight-thirty. His dream had pulled him in deeper than he'd imagined and lasted longer than he'd thought. This was rather late for him.

It was time for coffee and a shower. That would help.

He stood and stretched before meandering into the kitchen. If he were honest with himself, it seemed he had not fully released that dream state. Bleary-eyed, he went through the motions of starting a fresh pot of coffee.

Brianne loved the single serving makers, but he couldn't get on board with all that fancy coffee. He liked a good pot of basic grocery store brand. Nothing wrong with that.

As he started the coffee, he noticed that the TV was still on and Paul had fallen asleep on the couch. He reached for the remote but decided against it. The headlines scrolling caught his attention. More measures against the spread of the virus. Arguments about masking. And a coming vaccination.

Would he want to take a rushed vaccine? He wasn't so sure about that. Surely it would need to be thoroughly tested. That meant years, right?

But then, that might need to be another discussion with Brianne. She'd likely prefer he take it. There would be a weighing of options. He supported the concept of vaccines. Though there was reason to question one that had been thrown together so quickly.

Maybe.

Paul stirred, shifted, and started snoring. He'd been on the couch more and more of late. And, though he snored on his back, it wasn't so loud it bothered Scott when his door was closed.

He stepped back to the coffee pot. It had dripped out nearly six of the twelve cups. Grabbing his mug, he pulled the pot out— thankful for the 'sneak a cup' feature—and poured the dark brew. It smelled heavenly. A spoon of powdered creamer and he was good to go.

Paul's moan from the living room area startled Scott.

He glanced over and saw that his friend was starting to sit. And struggling to do so.

Probably still sleepy. Scott hoped he hadn't woken his roommate.

Maybe he could make it better by getting his coffee ready. So,

Scott pulled out another cup and poured the coffee then added a packet of Paul's chosen sugar substitute and a healthy dose of creamer.

He set his own mug down and walked Paul's to the coffee table. "Hey, man. You sleep well?"

Paul looked up at him with a confused expression. "Yeah. Did I fall asleep on the couch again?"

"Sure did." Scott bit back a laugh. But another look in Paul's direction stalled him out. The guy looked a bit like death warmed over.

A prickle of trepidation played at the edge of Scott's brain. No...Paul had just stayed up too late for the...um...not so early hour it had become.

"Here's your coffee." Scott scooted the steaming cup a little closer.

"Thanks." Paul yawned and, picking up the cup, leaned back into the couch. He did pull the throw blanket closer to him.

"You cold?"

"Yeah. What's the temperature in here?"

"Um..." Scott walked to the thermostat. "Seventy-three. Same as usual."

Another yawn was the only response. Then Paul brought the cup closer to his lips. Taking a big whiff of the caffeine elixir, he then sipped some.

But pulled it back as if he had gotten burned.

"Whoa...I just made it. Careful."

"Did we run low on ours? What brand is this?" Paul seemed genuinely confused.

And that bothered Scott. "It's the same as always."

Paul looked at his cup and then back at Scott. "Maybe it's the creamer or sugar." He took another, more careful sip. "Something leeched the flavor."

"Same creamer, same sugar...the pink one."

Paul's brows furrowed. "I can't taste it."

"The sugar?" Scott was becoming a bit nervous.

"No, the coffee." He leaned closer to the dark liquid. "I can't smell it either."

Was it possible? Scott backed away. "You sure you can't smell it or taste it?"

"No, dude. I told you. It's flavorless. Something is wrong with it."

Scott shook his head before he found his words. "It's the same."

"Whatever," Paul grumbled.

Scott ran into the kitchen and poured some lemon juice into a small cup. Then rushed it to the living room, and set it on the coffee table, careful to maintain as much distance as possible. "What about that?"

Paul picked up the glass and looked at it for a second. "What is this?"

"Just drink it." Scott's words were harsher than he'd meant. "Trust me."

"Okay," Paul downed the entire glass. No reaction.

Then Scott took another step back and worked to suppress the fear rising in him.

Paul had COVID.

*April 30, 2020*
*I-40 East*
*Waverly, TN*

Brianne stretched her arms as much as possible against the steering wheel. She was almost home. Maybe another hour, and she would be. It seemed strange that she was here. Out of her apartment and her comfort zone. But she was. The last couple of days had been filled with second guesses and resistance. Though, in the end, she knew that Scott, her parents, Latasha, and her counselor were right. It was time she stepped out in faith. Time she pulled back from the news—as scary as that seemed—and let God's plan work itself out.

Her bladder made its presence known. Not for the first time. It would be best if she could pull over at a gas station and go to the bathroom, but she was determined she could wait. That seemed an over-ask to avoid the coronavirus germs inside one of these stops. All those people, stopping, leaving behind viral calling cards. No, thank you.

She could make it. She was almost there.

Turning up her music, she attempted to distract herself from her bladder and from the thoughts swirling of all the risk she was taking.

No long after, her thoughts drifted to Scott. It was strange that he had not called her this morning. Or while she was on the road. Maybe he had back-to-back work meetings and was waiting on her call.

She'd stayed up late delving into his great grandparents' letters. They were sweet. But it was obvious Scott was trying to make a point about them surviving the pandemic of 1918. Perhaps she would accept that they could...and would...survive this pandemic. Maybe.

Besides, she hadn't had anyone close to her get sick. Then again, people were just now getting out again. Some brazenly risky. Some just to resume some semblance of normal life.

She purposefully hadn't asked her parents how much they had been out. Partly, she didn't want to know. And partly, she feared it would stymie her progress. And this drive was progress.

Going to her folks' home was progress. Every teeth-pulling, hand-forcing bit of it.

That wasn't something she wanted to dwell on. In truth, no one forced her, there were just really big nudges. But she had made the decision for herself.

The phone buzzed, and she glanced at it on its dashboard perch. Her mom.

She pressed the answer button on her car's screen. "Hey, Mom, couldn't wait one more hour to bother me?"

"Brianne..."

"I'm kidding, Mom. I know you worry. I've just passed the Waverly exit."

"Brianne, I need to tell you..."

"I know, be careful on the windy roads after Dickson. I will be, don't worry so. I've driven them a hundred times. I'll be fine."

"Brianne..." Her mother's voice was louder, harder somehow.

It gave her pause. "What is it?" Her heart fluttered with the possibilities of what her mother might need to say.

"It might be best if you pull over."

"Mom, you're scaring me." The wave of dread that washed over Brianne was much more than scared.

"Just do it, Brianne." It was a command. One of the kind her mother had not issued since she was a teenager.

"Yes, ma'am." Brianne spotted the next exit coming up. She pulled off the interstate to an eerie quiet from her mother. As soon as Brianne put the car in park in a gravel lot outside a gas station, she shifted to look at the car's screen. "What is it, Mom?"

"It's your father. He tested positive for COVID." Her mom's voice was shaky.

"No..." the word was whispered, but everything inside Brianne screamed. "When? How?"

"He just got the results a few minutes ago. Went to one of those walk-in clinics that does the rapid test."

"How long has he felt sick?" Brianne was near tears.

"Just since this morning. We wanted him to go ahead and test before you came home." Her mother's voice had firmed but sounded almost matter-of-fact. How was that possible?

"Are you isolating him?" Brianne hated to think of her mother, who was in weaker health than her dad, getting COVID as well. Or Lori...

"We are. The best we can. But the chances are that it has already spread."

"Listen, Mom, you have to clean the house, top to bottom. Keep him in the bedroom and only have him use that bathroom. You've got to keep you and Lori safe."

"I know..." Mom didn't sound convinced.

"You have to at least try. I can't..." She stopped herself. She wouldn't talk about anyone dying. Not her mother, her sister, *or* her father. Plenty of people recovered. Then again, many got sicker and ended up on a ventilator. "Is he breathing okay?"

"Yes. He just can't smell or taste as well as normal. And he's got a little bit of a fever and cold-like symptoms. Honestly, we thought that's all it was. Until he couldn't smell anything."

Brianne frowned and, steepling her hands, pressed her index fingers around her nose. "I...just don't know what to do."

"You have two choices, sweetie. You can come on home or you can go back to Memphis. We could sure use your help if we all get sick, but I don't want to risk you getting sick, too. So, I'll let you decide."

Brianne settled her head against the headrest. Such a decision. Which was the right one? For her? For her family? For all involved?

Her heart tugged her toward Clarksville and her family, but everything else bade her return to safety.

"I'll have to call you back, Mom."

"Okay. I understand." Her voice was almost muted. "Just know that we love you and support either decision you make."

"Thanks." Brianne almost whimpered the response. "I'll call you soon."

As she hung up, she was struck anew with the force of her full bladder. There was no way she would make it back to Memphis without a restroom stop. But if she risked that, she might as well head on to Clarksville and risk the germs there.

The urge to relieve herself was overpowering. She glanced over at the gas station. It seemed almost deserted. The only car in the lot probably belonged to the cashier. And this was a lone gas station in a small podunk area. Maybe...

Without another thought, she pulled on her mask and stepped from the car. She walked to the station and slipped inside. With only a head nod at the cashier, she moved toward the back of the store to the restrooms. Settling herself in her course of action, she stepped into the restroom, sanitizing her hands every minute or so through the process, and finished with a thorough wash of her hands and the faucet knobs.

Then she cleared the area, feeling guilty to not be making a purchase, but she just...couldn't.

She all but bathed her arms and hands in sanitizer at the car before getting in. And as she started the car, she couldn't remember feeling so gross.

But when she steered toward the interstate, she took the ramp toward Memphis. And prayed that her parents would understand.

# FOURTEEN
## *believing*

*August 25, 1918*
*Fort Campbell*
*Clarksville, TN*

*Dear Theodore,*

*Things have been difficult here. I can't quite express in words how trying and wearying it has become. Are you making progress? I pray every day that you can find a way to fight this thing. You are a capable physician and intelligent researcher. I believe if anyone can, you can...*

Theodore had read the letter many times. Rose's faith in him both bolstered and deflated him. Her support meant everything to him, but the fact that his research was getting nowhere was disheartening. More for what she was facing daily.

And he wondered, as he did so often between letters, how she fared now. What had happened between this letter and the one forthcoming? The communication between them, mostly on her side, had thinned somewhat. Not that he expected anything else with what they faced at Fort Riley.

He pulled out a fresh sheet of paper. Though she had yet to respond to his last letter, he would make every effort to encourage her anew.

*Dearest Rose,*

*I long for the day I can make a breakthrough. As of yet, I am only confirming how devastating and deadly this thing is.*

He hung his head. That wasn't encouraging. But it was real. Leaning over the paper again, he pushed on.

*My prayers are with you.*

"Dr. Hendry," someone said as they rushed to his door. It was the private that ran the communications for the building.

Theodore looked up at the intrusion. "Yes?"

"You have a phone call from Fort Riley. One of the nurses."

Theodore was on his feet in a moment. Rose! It had to be. Was it her on the phone? Or someone phoning that something had happened to her? Had she taken ill?

"I will follow you," he said to the younger man as he urged the private onward.

The walk to the telephone was long. And difficult. So many thoughts rushed through his mind. What would he do if Rose had become sick? Would his superiors allow him to return? Did it matter? Nothing could keep him from her. Of that, he was determined. Nothing.

He slipped into the more secluded area for calls and grabbed for the receiver even as a wave of apprehension overcame him, twisting his stomach. "This is Dr. Hendry."

"Theodore, it is good to hear your voice."

It was Rose. He closed his eyes and lifted a silent prayer of gratitude. "Yes, I'm relieved to hear from you. Are you well?"

"Yes. I am." The warmth of her voice flowed over him, soothing the ache that had developed in his chest. She was safe. She was well. He could breathe again.

"What..." He found that he struggled to speak. "Is there something you need?" Now that he had felt the depth of his despair in his fear, he knew he would move mountains if it meant she needed him.

"I just wanted to speak with you. There isn't time to send a letter before..." The last of her sentence became muffled.

"Rose? I didn't catch that last part."

She continued talking, but he couldn't make out her words.

"Rose," he called, hoping that she could hear him even if the connection was troubled.

"Theodore?" His name came through clearly.

"I didn't understand what you just said. You were muffled."

Silence. Was she still there? Just as he turned to seek out the nearby private, her voice sounded through the line.

"Are you still on the line?"

"Yes, darling, I'm here." He was so intent on her that the endearment slipped out.

"It's my family. My mother...and my brother. They have taken ill."

"Your family?" He realized he didn't know much about her parents or siblings. Not even where they lived. Or where she had grown up. "Is it...?"

"It's the Spanish influenza."

The pronouncement filled him with dread. Her family. What

would it be like for her to lose someone so close to her again? "I see."

"I've been given leave to go home."

No. She couldn't travel home. Wherever that was. He couldn't risk her. Not with things the way they were. With the flu spreading so rapidly. Living in close quarters with so many ill would put her at an even greater detriment. Could he convince her to stay put? Should he?

"Rose, I don't know if that's wise."

"What?" Her voice came through clearly that time. And it had an edge to it.

"What if you get sick on the way? Or contract it once you get there? There won't be anyone to tend you."

She was quiet for a few breaths. A seemingly endless pause.

"It's my family. I have to go. They need me."

He wanted to argue that he needed her. Needed her to stay put and stay well. But a part of him could discern his ridiculousness. She knew the risk. And it wasn't really his decision. "I understand that. Please...let me submit for leave. I'll come with you."

"You know that's not possible. Your work right now is important. So many need the answers you will find."

"But it's not more important than you." The statement rang out between them, halting their conversation and causing his heart to stutter.

After some moments, her gentle voice came on the line. "I appreciate that. But I won't let you sacrifice so many for me. Too many hospitals and medical wards will benefit from your research."

There was something else in her words. Something underneath. At least he thought he sensed that. Was there more she wasn't saying?

"I realize...I don't even know where your family is."

There was definitely a hesitation on the other end. "Illinois. A small town outside of Chicago."

He let out a breath. It wasn't that she wouldn't tell him. "When would you go?"

"I have my train passage booked for this afternoon."

"This afternoon?" How long had she known? How long had she planned this? Perhaps he wasn't to her what she was to him.

"Yes. It all happened so fast. And I wanted to tell you instead of write about it."

He was grateful for that, at least. It hadn't been her intention to delay telling him, then. But something whispered that there was more to this. Though what could that be?

"Does your father have a telephone? Might I ring you there?"

"No," she said on a sigh. "There isn't a telephone in the house. And I should quarantine with my family until they are better."

So she wouldn't be able to phone him from a nearby station.

"Can you tell me where I might direct letters? I will keep you posted on everything we discover. And...I want to hear from you."

"Of course." There was the tell-tale warmth of a smile in her voice.

She did care.

"I have to get off here now. There are others who need to make calls. And I have a little more packing to do."

His heart sank. He did not doubt the veracity of her statement, but he didn't like it all the same. "Be well, Rose. Be safe. And write me as often as you can."

"I will." There was that hint of tenderness again.

"And let me know if you have need of me."

She spoke, but it sounded almost as if she conversed with someone in the room. "Sorry, Theodore. They need the phone. I'll write soon."

Then the connection ended before he could say anything else.

He pushed out his displeasure on an exhale and shoved a

hand through his hair. Why did things always have to become so complicated? Laying the receiver onto the base, he stood and took several breaths. Anger, frustration, worry, and fear all fought for a dominant position in his heart.

But he couldn't let that happen. He had a job to do. And he would do it.

For her.

September 3, 1918
Garrett Family Home
Mendota, IL

Dearest Theodore,

I arrived some days ago. How many, I cannot say. One day blends into the next until I don't know what day it is. As horrid as the plague was on base, it is a whole different situation here. Caring for my mother and brother rips at my heart. They are so weak. And strug-gling. The doctor here has some rather unconventional approaches to tending for those afflicted with the influenza. I can only push back so much. I don't want my family to be his experiment. But my mother trusts him, so we shall see. I pray for the best either in response to or despite his efforts.

A knock at the door pulled Rose from the letter she should have long since written and sent. But duty called her from the task once more and she turned as her younger sister admitted Dr.

Peter Cooper. He offered Rose a winning smile as she stepped within.

"Clara, can you go let Mother know Dr. Cooper is here?" Rose waved her sister on. The younger Garrett sister had not shown any symptoms of the influenza. It was a miracle.

Her father was another story. He had some sputtering cough that concerned Rose, but he insisted he needed to work, or else the family had no income. But that stuffy factory was no place for him with the slight wheeze to his breaths.

"Dr. Cooper, I'm glad to see you." She offered him a small smile, it was the best she had at the moment.

"How is my favorite nurse?" He winked.

There were times that she wondered if he was being too kind. But he was highly credentialed and very much loved by the town at large. Besides, was there anything wrong with being a bit on the outgoing side?

She would reserve her judgment for later. Or until he did something untoward.

"I am about the same." She hoped the lines about her features didn't betray her fatigue too much.

"Are you taking care of yourself?" He frowned. All of a sudden, there was no joviality left. Only concern.

"As much as possible."

"You must take care. It will do your family no good if you were to get sick." His words were a bit stern. Not that she needed another person telling her what to do.

She nodded. "I will try, Doctor."

His eyebrows furrowed. "Try?"

"I will be more mindful." That was the best she could offer. Thankfully, it seemed to be what was needed for him to shift his focus.

"Now, let's look in on your mother and brother. Any changes since yesterday?" He was all business. The words they exchanged were but a distant memory. He held out a hand. "After you, Nurse Garrett."

She appreciated that Dr. Cooper addressed her as another person of medicine. But she did tire of being seen as a nurse. It was a role she chose for her work, yes. Yet it wasn't all she was. And she prayed Theodore saw more in her than that. He did, didn't he? She was certain it was so.

Rose led the doctor to the back of the small house, cramped all the more by setting aside a sick room. Her parents had precious little and their house held one bedroom, a modest living room, tiny kitchen, and an attic space that served as a bedroom for her siblings.

She had made herself at home on the couch and Father had taken to Silas's bed so they could keep Mother and Silas in the bedroom, as isolated as possible.

Dr. Cooper walked around her once they reached the room and rolled up his sleeves. "Tell me how she is."

"She is fevered and sleeps most of the day. There is somewhat of a raggedness to her breathing, too."

"It is probably time for a sponge bath."

Rose nodded. This was what she knew best—carrying out the doctor's orders. Not having to make decisions about what was best or what needed to be done. She could be a workhorse, determined and reliable. But having the weight of anyone's care solely on her shoulders? The thought made her shudder.

She moved off to collect the needed things.

He put out a hand to stop her. "Not just yet. Stay while I finish my examination."

Rose halted, only somewhat surprised by his touch. It proved he had attained a level of comfort with her. Maybe he should have a mind of taking care not to be more exposed than necessary.

He was diligent about washing his hands, especially before leaving the home. So, she should not fault him.

His hands moved over Mother, and he asked the older woman a few brief questions. None of which she answered.

Though Rose knew better than to respond for her. The doctor wanted to hear from Mother. Or not. But he didn't want Rose's interjections.

"Doctor," Rose ventured to a conversation they'd had before. But the way her mother burned with fever left her bereft of any other recourse. "Might we offer her something to ease the fever?"

He didn't bother to look at Rose. "No. Let the body do the fighting."

Rose wanted to shrug and throw up her hands, but she dared not. Mother had made her wishes quite clear days ago when she was more coherent. It was her desire that they give Dr. Cooper their service. He was in charge here.

"Shall I go for the water and sponge?"

He nodded, his face growing grim as he continued to work on Mother.

"What is it?" She refused to let the doctor avoid her or avoid telling her the whole of it. Perhaps he did not wish to speak of it in front of Rose's younger sister. "Clara, grab a basin and collect some water."

As the girl reluctantly grabbed the basin and obeyed, stepping from view, though likely not from earshot, Rose turned to Dr. Cooper again.

"What is it?" Rose's voice wavered a bit. Could she receive his prognosis and maintain a calm exterior? This was her *mother*. Perhaps not, but she would have it either way.

Dr. Cooper stood and moved to Rose. "I've done everything I can. But still, she regresses."

"Perhaps now we should try some aspirin to—"

"No," he said with a shake of his head. "I am no proponent of medication use when the body is well equipped to fight."

Rose chewed at her lip. There was certainly a time and place to add medicinals. If not now, when?

"Make sure she gets plenty of hot liquids. Broth as often as possible. And milk."

Dr. Cooper was an oddity in this day of medical wonders. The antithesis of Dr. Donovan, who was quick to give out anything that may aid in recovery. But Dr. Cooper's record of curing his patients—even during this pandemic—stood on its own.

"Yes, Dr. Cooper." And Rose wondered as she looked upon her mother's limp form if any of those making up his winning record had been so far gone as her mother.

The doctor moved toward Silas's makeshift cot and Rose looked away, hiding the fact that her tears had overwhelmed her ability to hold them back. What would become of her little family? Was there still hope?

FIFTEEN

*unexpected*

*April 30, 2020*
*QuikCare Clinic*
*Cordova, TN*

S cott watched the door to the clinic from his place in the
parking lot. Paul had gone in at least an hour ago. But the
parking lot was full. Who knew how long he would have to
wait for his COVID test?

Tugging at the uncomfortable mask, he lowered the cloth.
There was little reason to take precautions now that Paul had left
the car. Still, Scott lowered the windows to allow fresh air to
diffuse any lingering virus in the car interior.

He looked at his phone. A text from Paul detailed that he was
in the busy waiting room and that the lady at intake was not
quoting expected wait times.

You okay?

Scott tapped out to Paul.

> Yeah. Just tired of waiting. I'm pretty sure
> if I didn't have COVID before, I do now
> after sitting in here.

Scott didn't smile at the joke. It wasn't funny. There was little chance Paul hadn't walked in with COVID.

> Feel free to go hang out somewhere while
> I get tested.

But where would Scott go? He needed to be mindful of the fact he likely had COVID as well. With how contagious it seemed to be, there was little reason to doubt that.

Another ping. Goodness, Paul was insistent sometimes.

It was Brianne. In the craziness surrounding Paul's situation, he hadn't called her this morning. Or even texted. She was probably at her folks' by now.

> I'm almost back to Memphis.

The message stared at him from his screen.

What? Back to Memphis? Had she been too afraid to go the whole way to Clarksville? Scott didn't think he had it in him to convince her. The reality of his situation weighed on him like a heavy blanket. While he didn't believe the panic about COVID, some of the information was bound to be right. And the truth was, people were dying from it. Even people as young as him. There was no rhyme or reason to it apparently.

Then the thought struck him. How was he going to tell Brianne? She had so much on her already.

*No*, he told himself. He had made that assumption before and it led to a mistake. There was good reason to be open with her.

> Something has happened.

He took a deep breath. Yes, he would tell her, but he would ease into it.

> Yeah something happened. My dad has COVID.

Her father? That was why she came back. She couldn't be in the house with her dad's COVID. Oh, sweet Brianne.

> I mean something happened here.

He should come right out with it.

> Can I come to your apartment? I just don't want to be alone.

His heart fell. How cruel this situation was. She needed him, and he couldn't be there for her.

Yes, he needed to tell her right now. But not if she was driving. Surely she wouldn't be texting and driving.

> Where are you? Can we FaceTime?

He reached for the button to activate his FaceTime, but waited.

> I pulled off the interstate. I'm at a gas station near Arlington.

Just outside of Cordova. She was so close, yet unreachable.

He started to type a request to FaceTime again when his phone rang. An incoming video call.

Pressing the button, his breath caught when her face appeared on his screen. Her eyes were red and puffy. It wasn't a question in his mind—she had been crying. What else could he expect? Her father was sick. And he had other health concerns.

That tended to make things like COVID harder to get over. He wished he could reach through the screen, or tell her to come to him so he could hold her. But neither were viable solutions.

"Brie, are you okay?"

"No." Her reply was simple and almost curt. "I'm not. I need to see you."

"Oh, sweetheart. I'm afraid that's not possible—"

"What?" She cut in. "I didn't make it home. I wasn't exposed to my dad."

"It's not that." He wished that were all. "Believe me, I would put myself at risk to be able to be with you."

She sniffled and wiped her eyes. The hurt and confusion remained.

As much as he wanted to avoid the truth, or ease into it. There was no point. He had to be straight with her. "Brie, Paul has COVID."

She gasped and the color drained from her face. "Where are you?"

"I'm in the car outside the clinic. He is getting tested to be certain."

Her mouth moved, but no words came out. After a full minute, she finally spoke. "So there's a chance he doesn't have it."

"He has lost his taste and smell. And he has several flu-like symptoms. It's classic COVID." Scott was surprised she wanted to deny it.

"Did you ride in the car with him?" Her voice became hard edged.

"Yes. I wore a mask." Not that he truly believed his mask would do much, but it was something. "And I kept as much distance as possible. But you and I both know I've been exposed."

Her lips trembled. It broke him.

"But you can't...you can't get COVID." Her desperation was evident.

"Sweetheart, I assure you it's possible. And even more than that...likely."

She dropped her regard to the floor, but he saw her shoulders shaking. This was impossible—the distance between them, the fact that even if they were right in front of each other, he couldn't soothe her fears. Or even his own.

"What are we going to do?" Her reply came on a whimper. She did not look back at the camera.

"The only thing we can do." He swallowed. It was difficult with the thickness in his throat. "Trust God."

She pressed a hand to her face and her shoulders continued to shake. Would she trust God? Was she even capable?

Brianne couldn't stand to look at him anymore. It hurt too much. The thought that he might have COVID...that this may be...

She shook her head and pressed her hand to her mouth. Drawing in a deep breath, she tried to even her breathing and calm herself. This was not going to help her dad, or Paul, or Scott. No one would be aided by her emotional response.

Glancing back up as she blew out a lungful of air, she saw the raw ache in his features. This was difficult for him. And she wasn't making it any better.

"I...need to let you go." She pressed out on a shaky voice. "I have to figure out what to do."

"Brie, please don't go like this."

"Like what? I'm calm." She gave him the most tranquil exterior she could manage with breaths hiccupping out and her face a mess.

"Can we talk about your next move? I don't think you should to be alone in your apartment."

That was her decision, wasn't it? She sucked in a breath to tell him as much but stopped. This wasn't his fault. He only wanted to help. He cared for her. Loved her.

"Okay," she managed. Taking some more cleansing breaths, she tried to avoid thinking on the ramifications of the news she had received today. Another herculean task, but doable.

She thought of the verse in Philippians that talked about not being anxious for anything, repeating over and over what words she did remember.

"Why don't you call Latasha?" Scott's suggestion surprised her.

She hadn't really thought about that. With two people she loved in danger of COVID, she somehow thought it wasn't right to expose others. But she hadn't put herself in a vulnerable position. Unless one considered the stop at the gas station restroom.

Still, what weighed more...her need to be with a friend or the risk she had made herself susceptible to the virus?

The chance that she picked up the virus with all her masking and sanitizing was, in reality, not likely.

"Brie?" His voice was pleading.

"I'm thinking," she shot back. Then she quieted. "I'm sorry. It's just...a lot."

"I know. It's more than you should have to process all at once."

She nodded.

"But you are strong, Brie. I believe that."

That bolstered her a bit. She had been through a lot these last several years. Her mood disorder had taken her to the very edge of her life, and still God pulled her through. Why wouldn't He be able to do the same now?

She closed her eyes. Her spirit was weak and her desire to control had pressed her faith into uncomfortable places. Now that her breathing had started to even out, she looked to Scott's image once more. "Pray with me?"

He offered her a small smile. "Always."

Then he closed his eyes and prayed—over her father, over Paul, over both her and himself. For protection and endurance. And the ability to trust God's plan and timing.

Those were hard words, but words she needed and even *wanted* to believe. If she couldn't trust God, where was she? Nowhere.

He closed the prayer and then his dark eyes stared back at her. "Do you know what you need to do?"

She straightened her shoulders. "Yes."

He nodded but didn't ask her what that was exactly. His trust in her was life-giving. "Then don't hesitate."

She gave a quick nod. "I need to make another phone call."

"Of course. I'll let you know what happens here with Paul."

Her breath became uneasy again. But she stilled it. "I love you."

He lowered his lids slightly. "I love you more."

That made her smile. She made a kissing motion and ended the call.

Then she pulled up Latasha's number. And hit the call button. Unfortunately, her friend did not have FaceTime capabilities. So, old school would have to do.

"Hey, friend. It's been a while." Latasha's voice was bright and concerned. But that didn't mean judgment was being heaped on.

"Hey. I have a problem."

"Well, tell me what it is and we'll work it out together."

Brianne recounted the day and the events that had seemed to compound against her.

"You did the right thing by calling me," Latasha said on an exhale. "That is a lot, girl."

Brianne nodded. She wanted Latasha to know what she wanted without having to voice it. But that was silly. Brianne opened her mouth to speak, but Latasha beat her to it.

"Come on over here. The guest room is ready."

Brianne let loose her breath and the weight on her frame lifted. "You mean it? Your folks won't mind?"

"Mind? Who do you think made up the guest room? Certainly not me. I don't even know where Mom keeps the spare linens these days."

For the first time in a while, Brianne felt a sense of rightness about this direction. Even in the midst of her trepidation, a peace had settled over her spirit. She was done living in isolation. What had it gained her? Nothing. Her father was sick and so was Paul... putting Scott at risk. She had tried to do it her way, now it was time to trust. And despite the overwhelmingness of the circumstances, she could almost believe it was going to be okay. Almost.

*April 30, 2020*
*Trammel Apartments*
*Cordova, TN*

Scott drove the car into his designated spot and cut the engine. Then he looked at his friend in the passenger seat.

Paul had fallen asleep. It really had been a lot for him today. Between the long wait at the clinic, and the testing, and being sick on top of that.

But at least they knew for certain they faced a COVID diagnosis.

Scott had texted Brianne when the coronavirus infection was confirmed but had not heard back. Maybe he could try to video chat with her after getting Paul inside and settled. He needed a plan on how to care for Paul without putting himself at greater risk.

"Paul," Scott said, resisting the urge to touch his arm or shake his shoulder. The less contact, if any, the better for him.

Nothing.

"Paul, we're home," Scott said louder.

The guy jerked out of his slumber. "What?"

Scott frowned. "I said we're back. Let's get you inside and settled."

Paul nodded and shifted to open his door. He did not seem his usual self. But, then again, who would in his situation? There were some unknowns. And no doubt he just felt rough. He looked it.

Once inside the apartment, Scott set his keys in the designated spot on the bar and watched Paul move into the living room.

"Think you might be more comfortable in bed?" Scott hated that part of his motive was to have a chance to clean the apartment common areas and keep himself at as low a risk as possible. More difficult if Paul chose to set up camp in the living room.

"I'm good here." Paul plopped down on the couch.

Scott cringed.

Paul leaned back and reached for the remote but stopped himself. "Wait. I shouldn't stay out here, should I?"

Scott shrugged. He felt too guilty to say anything.

"You'd be less likely to catch it if I stay in my room."

Paul was not wrong. And Scott again hated himself for it.

"I think you'd be more comfortable there." Scott tried to avoid Paul's gaze, instead turning his attention to his phone.

"Yeah." Paul's words didn't sound convinced. Regardless, he stood and moved toward his room.

"Let me know if you need anything," Scott said as Paul reached his room's door. And he meant it. He would do whatever he could to help his friend beat this. But he would also have to be smart about it.

Paul nodded and slipped into his room, closing his door behind himself.

Scott deflated. He felt selfish. But was he? Or was this move just prudent?

His phone pinged. Glancing down, he saw that Brianne had finally responded.

> Thanks for letting me know.

He somewhat expected a frowning emoji. But none was there. Was she okay?

> How are you? Where did you end up?

> I'm at Latasha's. Getting settled.

Relief rushed through him to a degree he hadn't quite expected. She was safe...in more ways than just physical. Latasha would mother her in the ways she needed.

Scott wanted to collapse on the loveseat, but he dared not. At least not until he had thoroughly cleaned the living room. So, he went into his room and settled into his desk chair.

Then, and only then, did the full implications of his predicament settle in. COVID was real. And it wasn't a joke... despite the number of memes floating around social media. But he knew that people had to cope in a way that made sense to them. So he didn't begrudge the jokes. It just felt more real now.

Then it occurred to him...he would have to get groceries and supplies at some point. And...judging by his last check on bread... soon. Who should he call? Brianne seemed the obvious choice, but dare he ask her to push out of her comfort zone? Maybe his parents could help. He'd been texting with them today as well. His father was more level-headed about this whole thing than his mother. To hear her worries, one would think Paul was on his death bed.

He pulled his phone out again, determined to reach out to his father but paused. Should he not give Brianne the opportunity to help? It may be a positive thing for her. Though, he was certain he should not make decisions for her—either way.

So instead of clicking on his father's number, he pulled up the text thread with Brianne.

> Can you FaceTime right now?

Text bubbles. Then they disappeared. Then came back.

> Yes. Give me two minutes.

He glanced at the phone's clock and waited for the brief time to pass. Though it felt longer than a couple of minutes.

The time did tick by and he stretched his thumb to press the video call button when his phone rang.

She was reaching out to him.

"Hey," he said as he answered. Her face was bright on the screen. Such a difference from earlier in the day.

"Hey. How are you?"

She asked after him? That warmed his heart and gave him hope that she was able to see past her fear in the moment.

"I'm okay."

"Yeah?"

"Actually...I'm not sure I am."

"I get that. How is Paul?"

"About the same. He's in his room now. Hopefully resting."

She nodded. "Do you need anything?"

That stirred his heart as well. He had done the right thing reaching out to her first, giving her the opportunity to step in.

"Actually, yeah. But I can do grocery delivery."

"Nonsense. I can grab things for you curbside."

He smiled. His brave Brie, pushing past the difficult and into a solution.

"Want to send me a list?" She looked around as if searching for something. "You'll have to, I can't find my notebook anywhere."

"Sure. Are you comfortable there?"

"You bet. Latasha and her parents are so great. I wasn't eager to come over here, but now that I am somewhat settled, I know it was the right thing. I was only hurting myself by isolating." From the movement of the scenery behind her, he decided she had settled in a chair somewhere.

"Do you have everything you need? Or will you be heading back to your apartment?"

"I had packed for a longer stay in Clarksville, so I am set for a while I think."

Scott swallowed. There were many emotions swirling through his heart. About Brianne and her progress, about his risk, about Paul...it overwhelmed him. News facts plagued the edge of his mind...facts and stats about the virus. He had largely ignored them before, but they pressed at him full force now.

"You seem a bit distracted."

"I am. Just...thinking."

"Want to talk about it?"

"Not really. I want to hear about you."

She beamed. "I'm good. Really. This was absolutely the best thing."

"Good. I'm proud of you for doing the hard thing."

"Thanks." She looked down.

Had he said something he hadn't meant to? Like called her ugly or something? He could be a bonehead about those things sometimes...tripping over words trying to express his heart.

"Hey. I didn't mean to say that you aren't—"

She waved him off. "No worries. I was just thinking."

"About your dad?"

She nodded. "And Paul. And you. It worries me. But I'm not paralyzed with fear anymore. Somewhere along the way, I started listening...to you...and my counselor. And looking for God to be faithful instead of expecting the worst."

That eased Scott's whole being. "I'm glad. Maybe it's my turn to be apprehensive."

She shook her head. "Not you."

He offered the best smile he could, which felt weak. How could he tell her that fear was gripping at him?

"I think the praying has made a difference for me."

"Good."

"Maybe we should do that more often."

He sighed. It was a wonderful thing, but he didn't feel much like praying in that moment. His thoughts were so clouded by concern over what was—and may—happen. But maybe this was a chance for him to lean on her a little?

"Do you..." he cleared his throat. "Do you think you could pray now?"

The moment felt more vulnerable than he'd expected.

Her features softened even as she seemed to hesitate. "Of course."

Scott closed his eyes as she began and let her words wash over him, begging silently that God would help the uneasiness and budding distrust within him.

And then he rested in her words.

SIXTEEN

*thief*

*September 12, 1918*
*Garrett Family Home*
*Mendota, IL*

*Dearest Rose,*

*It has been quite some time since I have received word from you. It gives me cause for concern. I am certain your days are filled with many things related to caring for your family, but I worry about you. I hope you are well…*

R ose pinched the bridge of her nose as the words blurred together. The letter was a week or so old and she had yet to respond. Even if she wanted to write back now, her head ached. The strain of the last several days—both physically and emotionally—had taken its toll. And she was feeling the effects of it.

183

Clara stepped into the room and brought a hot cup of tea to where Rose sat at the table, the room so silent that the gentle *thunk* of the mug hitting the table seemed loud.

"Thank you." Rose didn't look up from her hunched position. Though she did ache for her sister. This must be incredibly difficult for her. She was too young to face the prospect of losing her mother.

Rose was too young, for that matter.

She sipped the tea and it served to calm her stomach somewhat. But what could be done to revitalize her body? All of her seemed sore. Yet the needs levied upon her did not change. In fact, they had continued to worsen. Her father had been too ill to even stand this morning. So the sickroom had been increased by one.

Rose fought the urge to dwell on that. The emotion sank in enough without her chasing the feelings into a dark place she dare not venture.

She was fighting this flu with everything she had. And had been for months—first at Fort Riley, then here. Yet she continued to lose battles to the invisible foe.

It didn't matter, she reminded herself. The battles didn't matter as long as she won the war ultimately.

The war that she waged here was certainly a smaller scale than the war that still ravaged the globe. And the spread of the flu made it all the worse. More and more became sick. More and more fell—soldiers and civilians alike—to its grip.

A hand fell on her shoulder.

She jerked her regard to the side. It was just Clara. Strong, brave Clara.

"You should rest," came her small voice. Though a firmness laced her tone.

"I will. I just...need to check on Mother's fever."

Clara pulled out her flu mask. "I will do that. You need rest."

Rose wanted to argue but couldn't find the strength. So, she nodded. She gulped down the remainder of the tea and moved toward the couch.

Clara stood in the kitchen and watched until she settled. Only then did the thin girl move off into the bedroom.

Rose was a failure. She shouldn't let Clara do these things. It was imperative that Rose limit Clara's exposure. But she couldn't make herself rise. Maybe it wasn't the worst thing to lean on her sister for a little bit.

Even as she lay and tried to quiet her mind, sleep was fitful and elusive. She dozed and woke and slept and jerked awake. It all seemed hazy.

A presence bent over her.

She tried to get up but couldn't make her body obey. Opening her eyes into mere slits, she noted that it was a man. Perhaps the doctor.

"Rose," the voice said. It sounded so far away. As if it traveled through water. "I'm here, Rose."

She forced her lips to move. "Dr. Cooper?"

The blurry figure looked away and called across the room. Another form, perhaps Clara, came closer. And the two conversed.

Soon enough, she was being lifted. Strong arms carried her through the small house. And she breathed in a familiar scent. Theodore? Yes, the spiced sandalwood was something she associated with him.

But it couldn't be him. He was miles away, working to cure this illness. He wouldn't be here. He couldn't be.

The masculine scruff of his chin brushed against her forehead.

"I've got you." The words were the clearest she had heard yet.

She did so much want to melt into him. To let him carry her to a place where this influenza didn't exist. Where she could be Rose and he could be Theodore. And there would be all the time in the world for the two of them.

But she was placed on a softer surface and then his arms retracted.

"No..." she moaned. Trying desperately to cling to him.

To no avail. He was gone.

And she was falling, deeper and deeper into nothingness.

*September 13, 1918*
*Garrett Home*
*Mendota, IL*

Theodore watched Rose sleep. She looked so peaceful, so angelic. Her dark hair fell in waves on the pillow. And her pale skin had a rosy hue to it. But that was the problem—she suffered from a high fever. A fever he was mostly powerless against. A thief that may well snatch her away. Forever.

Rose's sister, whom he had come to know as Clara, came in the room.

"How is she?"

He shook his head. These people were strangers to him. But they were Rose's family. And he would care for them. "I think she is worse."

Clara frowned. "Perhaps I should sponge her off."

"That would help." Until he could get some medicine to bring the fever down, that was best.

Clara grabbed for the basin and left the room, but he heard her movements to the kitchen and the gentle splashes as she filled the bowl with fresh water.

What else could he do?

Rose's mother and brother seemed somewhat improved. At least they had been coherent for parts of the night. No doubt their fevers would break soon. And that would signal an end of the worst of it for them.

But not necessarily for Rose. He knew all too well that the age bracket she was in tended to be afflicted the most.

Clara was back in the room before he realized. She stood silently behind him.

"Please, don't let me stop you." He glanced at her briefly before setting his sights back on Rose.

"I...don't know that it is becoming for you to be in the room."

"I am a doctor," came his incredulous response. "It is perfectly acceptable." Though as he looked at Clara's wide eyes, his defensive flare subsided and he knew she was not wrong. Of course he shouldn't be in the room. "My apologies, you are right."

He dragged himself to his feet, his body slowed more by emotional weariness than the lack of sleep the night before as he cared for the family.

"There is a fresh pot of coffee in the kitchen." Clara's voice was small, hesitant almost.

That was his fault. There had been no reason for him to speak to her so harshly before. Certainly not when she only protected her sister's modesty.

"Thank you." It was the only thing he could manage. He moved toward the bedroom doorway, wanting so much to apologize again, but not sure how to.

So much about this situation was new to him—the risk of losing someone he loved, the all night caregiving, even his own reaction. In the end, he decided it would be best to talk to Clara later and let her get to her task right now.

Lord knew Rose needed something—anything—to calm her fevered body.

After closing the bedroom door behind him, he removed his mask, stepped into the kitchen, and stumbled to the counter. A mug waited for him. Which he quickly filled with steaming coffee.

It was incredibly hot, but he sipped it anyway. Something had to wake him up.

He settled into a dining chair at the small table and looked around. Everything about the house was small. Every room, every surface. Nothing like what he was used to. Was this where Rose grew up? He found it strange once again that they had professed such deep feelings for each other, yet knew so little about each other.

Had it been a mistake to speak those words so soon? He had felt them. Yet was there the depth that was needed to make for a solid foundation?

He continued to sip his coffee.

Sounds from the bedroom drew his attention. A woman groaned. Rose? Was she hurting? But Clara would take care, wouldn't she? Perhaps he should have put on his professional air and remained to assist.

There were other voices. One that soothed and one that questioned. Clara was a natural caregiver, like her sister. The first voice was likely hers. The other...was it Mrs. Garrett? Awakened again? Or was it Rose?

Could Rose have come around enough to ask questions?

He moved to the door and listened.

The rougher voice sounded older. Raspy, but older. So, likely it was Mrs. Garrett.

He turned to claim his seat once more. But then Rose called out. It was a muted, quiet sound, but distinctive.

"Dr. Cooper?"

That chipped at him. Had something developed between her and the local physician? Such that she would call for him in her delirium?

Perhaps she only sought to speak with him? But Theodore knew he was making excuses. She had called for Dr. Cooper yesterday when he had found her limp, burning form on the couch.

What would he do if that was true? If she had feelings for this other doctor? Then something in him resolved to seek her happiness...whatever that may mean. Not that it didn't pain him. Indeed, it was as if a poker had shot through his chest. But he would be all right as long as she lived.

He deflated into the chair once more and dropped his head into his hands. *God, I promise...I won't be selfish about keeping Rose. If only Your mighty hand would fall on her now and rescue her from this plague.*

The prayer even stung. Shouldn't he have made more progress with a cure? Or a treatment? Maybe that was God's intention. Then he would have been able to help Rose now. Had he erred or sinned in some way?

A knock on the front door startled him.

He looked in that direction as if he might see who had come. But, of course, he couldn't.

Glancing at the bedroom door, he wondered if Clara had heard it as well. If she may appear soon and answer it. Or should he?

She was rather busy at the moment. Still, he was a guest here, not a member of the family.

The knocking continued.

He couldn't let it go until whomever it was disrupted the care of the sick. Rising once more, he walked toward the sound. As the knocking became louder and more insistent, he bit back his words to beseech the guest to be mindful.

Soon enough, he was at the door. He had the thought that he should pull his mask back on and did so before opening the door.

A man stood just outside. His brow furrowed at the sight of Theodore. Yes, probably rather unexpected.

"Be mindful," Theodore warned the man. "There is Spanish Flu in this house."

"I know it all too well, sir." The man stepped forward as if he intended to enter.

Theodore blocked his path. "I should caution you again."

The man waved a hand. "There is no need. I am the family doctor."

Theodore froze and when he regained his tongue, hazarded a guess. "Dr. Cooper?"

# SEVENTEEN

## *gripping*

*May 5, 2020*
*Leyton Home*
*Bartlett, TN*

Brianne set another letter to the side and lay back against the pillow on the guest bed. Poor Rose. Her pain was shakingly familiar as Brianne's father fought the coronavirus. His asthma made things more difficult. And made Brianne more worried.

Rose seemed a little lost in her weariness. What must it have been like to care for so many that were ill? To lose friends? A fiancé?

Brianne's throat tightened at that thought.

*No,* she told herself. *Scott will be fine. Even if he gets sick...he is strong and young. He will beat this.*

Holding onto that, she sighed. It felt empty though. She could no more command Scott's survival than Rose could her mother's and brother's. It was up to God.

Latasha's laugh carried through the warm home and into the guest room.

Brianne had left the door open so she could still feel like a part of the family. She was so grateful for Latasha and her friendship. And her family opening their home.

Both work and counseling had continued without interruption. Latasha and her family had their own responsibilities. Thankfully, none that took them outside of the home, save the run for goods.

Which was stretching Brianne's comfort level, but no longer in a way that was painful. She'd even made the grocery grab for Scott. And that, too, had been fine.

It had been a while since she'd heard from Scott. Not since yesterday morning. Had she so lost track? Or was this evidence that he took charge of keeping in touch more than she?

Picking up her phone, she typed out a text.

> Working through your great grandparents' letters. I didn't know how bad the Spanish flu was.

She waited.

Nothing.

She pinged him again.

> How are you today?

Nothing.

Maybe she should give him a minute. So, she sat up and slid the last letter read carefully into its envelope.

Her hair fell in waves around her. Maybe she was due a haircut. How would that be? Would her hairdresser be open? Where did they fall in the order of necessary businesses?

Latasha's laughter grew and multiplied. What was so funny?

Glancing at her phone screen once more, Brianne tried not to let her mood slump at the lack of response. He might be sleeping, for goodness sake. Just because he wasn't texting back didn't automatically mean he was holed up dying.

Gathering herself, she hopped up off the bed and walked to the family's living room.

Latasha and her brother were playing a game. There were cards on the table and weird plastic contraptions in her brother's mouth. He tried to talk despite that. It was strange.

The next laugh that belted out was her own. His attempt was just so comical.

Latasha and Donnell jerked toward her.

"Sorry." She shook her head.

Latasha waved her hand. "Donnell is a jokester. No apologies necessary. He's had my side splitting for the last hour."

"I know. I heard it."

"You weren't working, were you?"

Brianne opened her mouth, but Latasha continued, slapping a hand over her mouth in horror. "Oh no, you were in a video conference!"

"No," Brianne laughed then at the picture Latasha made. "Nothing like that. Just doing some...reading."

"Oh? Anything good?"

Donnell took the plastic thing out of his mouth and gathered his cards.

"Yeah. Rather interesting."

"Oh, you'll have to tell me all about it later," Latasha said before shifting her focus back to her brother. "So you're giving up?"

"No." Donnell grinned. "I can't very well play with someone who won't stop laughing like a hyena."

"Only because you make it impossible to keep a straight face with your crazy self." Then Latasha shot a look at Brianne. "Want to play?"

"I've never been much for these kinds of games." Brianne shrugged. "But I play a mean game of spades."

Latasha's eyes lit up. "Donnell, go get Ma, and we'll see what's what with her spade talents."

Brianne grinned. "You're on."

Donnell shoved the cards he had gathered back into the game box and took his mouthpiece thing with him. Hopefully to drop it off in the kitchen to be cleaned.

"Sit," Latasha commanded as she patted the chair next to her.

The table only had room for four. This was likely where the family had typically eaten. It was less formal than the table they'd been having dinner at since Brianne came. But they had five people here now. They wouldn't all fit at this smaller table.

"Any word from Scott? How is Paul today?"

Brianne settled into the offered seat. "Funny you should ask. I texted him a little bit ago and..." She pulled her phone out again, glancing at the screen before holding it up to Latasha. "Nothing so far."

"Maybe he's in his coding world. He sure can get hyper focused." Latasha spoke with confidence, but Brianne sensed she held something back.

It was true that Scott could get so intent on his work he could block the world out. Maybe that was all there was to it. "Thanks, friend. I needed to hear that."

"You got it. Any time you need the voice of reason, I'm your girl." She flashed Brianne a brilliant smile. "But I gotta say..."

Would she not finish? Brianne waited with bated breath.

"Scott has been awfully strong for quite some time."

That gave Brianne pause. While Latasha wasn't wrong, Brianne wondered if she meant more by that statement.

Latasha laid a hand over Brianne's. "You may find there could be a chink in that suit of armor. I pray that you'll be able to be strong for him."

Brianne blinked. Of course she would be there for Scott. She loved him. But there was something about Latasha's words that hit a vulnerable spot in her. Something for her to ponder later.

There was movement in the direction of the kitchen. No doubt Donnell and Mrs. Leyton were headed this way.

"Sounds like that spades game may be a go," Latasha announced, pulling her hand back and looking in the same direction. "You gonna play it safe and be my partner? Or risk it with Donnell?"

"Why can't I be your mom's partner?" Brianne tilted her head and crossed her arms, putting on a defiant air.

Latasha shook her head. "Oooh no. That's too much of a shoe in. I don't want to just hand over the win."

Brianne lit up. "Okay. I'll partner with you, then."

Latasha leaned toward her and with a lowered voice, said, "That's best. Give Donnell the greatest chance to make something of his limited skill."

Brianne had to bite her lip to keep from laughing. Latasha could pick at her brother, but they both knew she adored her younger sibling.

"Now, move over to that chair." Latasha indicated the seat across the table from herself. "Hurry, before they decide for you."

Just then, Brianne's phone vibrated. She picked it up from the table surface and glanced at the screen.

"What is it?" Latasha asked. "Is it Scott?"

Brianne was frozen. There must be some mistake. Or she was reading this wrong?

"Brianne?" Latasha urged, her voice rising. "Everything okay?"

Looking at her friend, Brianne could do little else than hand her phone over.

"Paul is in the hospital?" Latasha's likewise disbelieving voice declared. "This is real?"

Brianne took her phone back. Indeed it was.

"Excuse me," she muttered as she sprinted back to the guest room.

"Brianne," Latasha called after her.

But she didn't follow. And Brianne was grateful for that. It was too much. This thing had become bigger than she could handle.

And she couldn't pretend anymore.

*May 5, 2020*
*Saint Francis Hospital*
*Bartlett, TN*

Scott leaned over his steering wheel. How had this gone so terribly wrong? And so quickly? He beat his fist against the dashboard. It was too much. Hadn't he carried on enough? When would it be his turn to rest?

His phone pinged. He wanted to ignore it. This was all too much.

But it was probably Brianne. And he wouldn't avoid her. No matter how heavy his burden seemed.

Though as he picked up his phone, he saw that it was Latasha's contact flashing at him. Had something happened to Brie?

He swiped up to activate the phone so he could read the message.

> I am so sorry to hear about Paul.

Sighing, he wanted to put the phone back down. Of course she was. Everyone was...including him. Deeply sorry.

But he had to make Brie a priority over his own guilt at his failings. So he typed out a quick text.

> How is Brianne?

> As expected. She shut herself in the guest room.

He couldn't handle this. How was he supposed to be there for her when he had to be quarantined? How could he reach out when he had nothing left to give?

He couldn't. Plain and simple.

Then he remembered their new habit of praying together. Was that what he should do? Pray?

He attempted to clear his thoughts so he could form cogent words. But none came. Nothing but anger. How was he supposed to live a life that was pleasing to God if there were such obstacles?

Then again, the Bible promised trials. And Scott knew well enough that it wasn't the absence of problems that made one's faith. It was the endurance through them.

Something only accomplished with God.

Yes, he knew all of that, but still he couldn't make himself pray. So, he trusted that the Holy Spirit would plead for him.

Leaning on the steering wheel again, he took several breaths. And though nothing around him changed, there was some peace stilling the storm within.

Another ping sounded.

> We'll take care of Brianne. Do you need anything?

Latasha's words were kind. A balm of sorts. He did have need of prayers and support and...so many things. It was difficult to narrow it down to something tangible.

> I'm headed back to the apartment. Just pray for Paul's recovery.

> Will do. And for your protection from the virus.

A smile tugged at his lips. Yes. Protection for him. His own wellbeing was the last thing on his mind. But it was important.

He turned off the phone screen and made a move to shift gears when another ping caught him. What now? The reality of his impatience wore on him.

It was Brianne. He switched the car into park.

> I'm trying to pray. But I'm worried.

> I know. I am too.

His own honesty surprised him. Yet there was an element of that needed in their relationship—his honesty. His openness about his own struggles.

The phone rang. He stared at it curiously. It wasn't like Brianne to initiate a call when they were already texting.

It was Paul's mother's number.

Scott answered, a dread falling over him. "Hello?"

"Hello, Scott. Mrs. Collins here."

"Yes. Hello." He didn't bother to remind her that her contact name flashed up the second she called.

"I wanted to thank you for taking Paul to the hospital. They've admitted him and are talking about a ventilator but haven't resorted to that yet."

"I see." The ventilators seemed to be the last ditch effort these days. And those that went on them rarely came off. None of that would be constructive reminders right now.

"We'll keep you posted as they tell us anything." The woman's voice caught. "They won't let us come see him."

"I know. And I'm sorry."

"Thank you. Paul has always been so thankful for your friendship."

Scott set his head against the headrest. He didn't want to hear this. It wasn't time to share these kinds of things. There was hope still, wasn't there? "I am grateful for him, too. And I will keep praying."

"Thank you. Let us know if you need anything. How much longer is your isolation?"

"Another two weeks from my last contact with Paul."

"Okay. Just let us know."

"All right. Thanks. You do the same."

The woman sniffled, said a brief good-bye, and ended the call.

Scott had a thought. There were some experimental medications being used for COVID, weren't there? Monoclonal something or another. But the mainstream media was not a fan. And most medical facilities would not use them off label. Would Paul's doctor try it if nudged?

He opened his eyes and stared at the ceiling of his car. It wasn't his decision. Or his place. And that was hard—the lack of control he had over the situation.

Then it struck him. He had talked to Brianne about her urge to control her environment and risk. But was he doing the same thing? Only in a different way? Was he trying to tell God what needed to happen? Relying on God to do his bidding like some sort of cosmic genie?

As a pang tore through his heart, he knew it was true. His reliance only looked like real faith on the outside. But he was just as scared as Brie and just as quick to lean on his own understanding. Just because it looked different didn't mean it wasn't so.

*God,* he started, not sure what to say. Yet the words came. *I am sorry for treating You like that. For leaning on myself and believing I was trusting You. Help me see the places where I am doing this and redeem it as only You can.*

He prayed the words over and over. They weren't eloquent or especially holy sounding. But they were real. Raw. And exactly what they needed to be.

*May 5, 2020*
*Leyton Home*
*Bartlett, TN*

Brianne turned the crinkling page of her Bible. After her latest text with Scott, she could do nothing other than turn to God's word and hope for comfort.

She started in Philippians 4 with the passage about being anxious. Then she was drawn to Isaiah 43. The instruction not to fear was coupled with imagery about passing through fire and not being burned and through water without being swept under. Both fantastical ideas. Both brought to reality. God carved a pathway through the sea for the Israelites fleeing Egypt. And He preserved Shadrach, Meshach, and Abednego in the fire.

Did He perform miracles like that today? She had herself experienced Him reaching out to still her hand when she wanted to injure herself. If that wasn't miraculous, what was it?

*Oh, God, help me see. Help me believe like this.*

There was a knock on the door.

She sighed. It was only a matter of time. She had been shut up in here for at least an hour. It surprised her no one came sooner.

"Yes?" she called. But she knew who it was.

"May I come in?" But it wasn't Latasha's voice. It was Mrs. Leyton.

Brianne glanced around to ensure there were no messes to find in their guest room and straightened herself out, sitting up a bit straighter and pushing her hair off her shoulders.

"Yes. Of course."

The door creaked open and Latasha's mother slipped in, leaving the door mostly closed. "I understand you're in a bit of a pinch."

Brianne nodded and resisted the urge to wipe at the gathering moisture in her eyes.

The woman set her eyes on the Bible in front of Brianne. "Well, it looks like you found the right place to go." She stepped farther into the room and quoted, "I will lift up mine eyes unto the hills, from whence cometh my help. My help cometh from the Lord, which made heaven and earth."

Brianne nodded and looked down, unable to face the woman's tender features anymore. All of her fear hurt and guilted her too much.

"Oh, Brianne, it's all right to be upset. Trusting God doesn't mean we don't have emotions. Or the need to express them." Mrs. Leyton sat on the side of the bed nearest Brianne's chair.

Brianne bit at her lip to keep it from trembling.

"You're in a tough spot. People you love are hurting. They are sick. And there isn't anything you can do about it." She tried to catch Brianne's downturned gaze. "Right?"

Brianne nodded again, not trusting her voice.

"My mother was a godly woman. And when she was diagnosed with cancer, it was hard for me. It was a journey, and nothing less, to come to terms with it. And with God."

Brianne looked up. She hadn't known that Latasha's grand-mother had walked that road.

"There wasn't anything easy about it. And there aren't any shortcuts. Not even the ones we try to carve out."

And goodness, Brianne had been trying to make her own way here.

"You know what my mother said to me in the midst of that pain and anger?"

Brianne shook her head.

"Lean not unto thine own understanding. In all thy ways acknowledge Him, and *He* shall direct thy paths."

Brianne was familiar with the passage. It had been the first verses she memorized. Her own grandfather had taught her this well enough.

"That means that we don't make the path and we don't keep the path. Only He can. He invites us to walk it with Him as our guide, aid, friend, and master. Nothing less."

Brianne knew God was Almighty and Lord of everything. But did she really think of Him as a friend and guide?

"Tell Him what you feel. Trust Him to help you hold those emotions."

Brianne couldn't help the tears that started to fall. Was it really so simple? But He was the God of the universe. How could she tell Him about her doubts and fears? Wasn't that the same as questioning Him?

Mrs. Leyton reached out a hand and set it on Brianne's. "Supper will be ready in about an hour. If you need to talk, you know where to find me."

Mrs. Leyton rose and walked toward the door.

"Mrs. Leyton?" Brianne called, tears now fell openly down her face.

The older woman turned. "Yes?"

What did she want? The thought on the tip of her tongue

sounded strange to her, but she had to try it. "Would you sit with me while I pray?"

"Of course, dear." Mrs. Leyton came back around the bed and sat on the edge once more. Then she bowed her head. She did not speak nor did she seem to expect Brianne to.

Brianne closed her eyes and prayed silently, seeking understanding, a right view of who God was to her, and for peace on this journey.

# EIGHTEEN

## *uncertain*

*September 13, 1918*
*Garrett Home*
*Mendota, IL*

Theodore stared at the physician standing in the doorway. He didn't know what to say. This was Dr. Cooper? The man was younger than he'd expected. It caused his ire to burn a bit hotter.

"And who might you be, sir?" Dr. Cooper asked.

The man had nerve. Did he imply that Theodore had no business being here?

Theodore took a step back and tried to calm himself. The man was not saying any such thing. It was just Theodore's jealousy overriding his good sense.

"I'm Dr. Theodore Hendry. I worked with Rose and..." He wanted to say more, but what? How to describe his relationship with Rose?

Dr. Cooper's eyebrows lifted as if he waited for the remainder of that statement.

"And I'm here to help in any way I can."

Dr. Cooper smiled. "I appreciate it. We can use all the expertise we can get. All hands on deck, as it were."

The man stuck out his hand and smiled. Smiled. At Theodore.

Dismissing his trepidation, Theodore gripped Dr. Cooper's hand and gave it a shake.

Then Dr. Cooper slid past Theodore and into the house. "Where is Rose?"

The man's use of her given name frazzled Theodore even more. "She has taken ill."

Dr. Cooper's features became lined. "She has? When?"

"Yesterday afternoon. Clara and I moved her into a bed in the sickroom."

"Good." Dr. Cooper's features were still downcast. Did the man have more of a care for Rose than he should? "What are her symptoms?"

"She was largely non-responsive when I arrived. But she burned with fever and seemed somewhat delirious." She must have been to have called out for Dr. Cooper. Or so, Theodore hoped.

"Take me to her." Dr. Cooper slid his flu mask out of his pocket and stepped out of the door's path.

Theodore closed it soundly and watched Dr. Cooper, ensuring the man got his mask secured before they moved on.

He led Dr. Cooper to the bedroom door. But at the last second, he remembered Clara was sponging off Rose. So he knocked.

"Clara, Dr. Cooper is here to see to the sick."

"All right," came her faint response. "I'll be done in a minute."

Great. He was stuck out here with Dr. Cooper. With nothing to say.

Though, after a few moments of awkward silence, the physician spoke. "You worked with Rose at Fort Riley?"

"Yes. Briefly." Why had he volunteered that added information?

Dr. Cooper nodded. "Are you based there?"

"No." Theodore considered how much to share. Was there a reason to withhold information? "I'm stationed at Fort Campbell. More for research than tending patients."

"You've been doing research?"

"Yes. Trying to find answers for this pandemic."

"Oh?" The man became a bit more intrigued. "Any progress?"

Theodore wished he hadn't said so much. For he was ashamed to admit how little he had accomplished. He had just opened his mouth, when the door opened.

Clara stared at the two men, her face wane and tired.

Theodore would have to make sure she rested today.

"Good day, Clara," Dr. Cooper said. "How are they?"

She glanced between Theodore and Dr. Cooper. "Mother is much improved. She's awake right now. Silas, too, has stirred in the night a few times and doesn't feel as hot to the touch."

Dr. Cooper nodded. "Wonderful news." His voice had taken on a warm quality.

It tugged Theodore a bit farther from his anger toward the man.

"Let's check on your mother first." Dr. Cooper nodded to Clara and followed her further into the room.

Theodore stood for a moment, trying to decide if he should join them, and then proceeded as well. If he was helping care for the family, he needed to be privy to the state of things. Things they may be more open to say to their town physician than to a virtual stranger such as he.

He watched Dr. Cooper take a seat by Mrs. Garrett and examine her. She answered his questions, tossing a look at Theodore every now and again as if she didn't quite trust him.

Dr. Cooper looked in that direction then said to Mrs. Garrett, "I'm sure you met Dr. Hendry. It's a good thing he will be here to help with your care. Especially with Rose unwell."

The woman looked more closely on Theodore than she had and seemed decided to trust Dr. Cooper.

In this, Theodore was thankful for the man. It would be better if the family members trusted him.

Dr. Cooper finished with her and then moved to Silas, who stirred as the man started his work.

Just as with Mrs. Garrett, Silas appeared to be much improved from yesterday. As well, he was more confused by Theodore's presence than comforted.

It mattered little to Theodore, he told himself. He was here for Rose.

They then shifted to Mr. Garrett. His fever had continued to climb. From 102 yesterday, it was up five tenths. He was not out of danger yet. Still, he appeared to fare better than Rose.

Theodore glanced to where she lay. Clara had sponged her and changed Rose's nightdress. But there was little sign about her that she had any awareness at all.

Soon enough, Dr. Cooper stepped to where Rose lay, sweat beading on her forehead from the heat of her body. Dr. Cooper took her temperature. He then looked to Theodore.

"103 and eight tenths."

Theodore frowned. It was all he could do to swallow his words of worry. He had to keep himself together.

Dr. Cooper asked Clara some of the same questions he had in relation to the others. Their conversation continued longer than Theodore could stand it. Would the man do nothing to really help Rose?

"Dr. Cooper, if I may..." he started.

The man looked up from his chatting with Clara. "Yes?"

"I hoped you might have some fever pills that we might use to bring down this climbing temperature."

Dr. Cooper frowned. He glanced at Clara and then back at Theodore. "I do not carry such medicine."

"What? Not even aspirin? How do you expect to treat fevers? Or other symptoms?" This was outrageous.

"I more prefer to let the body combat the sickness. The heat is more than just a fever, as you well know. It is the body fighting the ill within. I have no desire to interrupt or shortcut that process. We can maintain natural remedies for the symptoms without interfering with what the immune system is doing."

Theodore was certain his mouth hung open. And he was thankful his mask kept Dr. Cooper from seeing it.

When he found his voice, he spoke up. "You cannot be serious. This flu is killing hundreds. And quickly."

Dr. Cooper's eyes shone with compassion, but he shook his head. "I'm sorry, but that is my preference."

"Then I will secure some myself and see to Rose and her father's care."

Dr. Cooper stood. "I am their physician. I wish to handle it this way. It is best that we don't contradict each other in treating this flu."

Theodore took a step back. "I daresay I would have Rose's blessing to proceed how I see fit."

"That may be. But she is clearly not able to speak for herself. So, we don't know."

The man had a gentle way about him despite his crazy solution. Theodore hated to be on the attack, but this was Rose. It mattered how they treated her illness.

"What, then? We are at an impasse." Theodore grunted. This man could not control what Theodore did after the good doctor left.

Dr. Cooper sighed and then looked to Mrs. Garrett. "We must let her mother decide. She is her next of kin."

Theodore's eyes widened as he settled his gaze on the older woman. This was impossible! The woman didn't know him and clearly didn't trust him. How could he stand for this?

Dr. Cooper stepped around the bed and closer to Mrs. Garrett. "Ma'am, it is up to you how we approach treatment for your daughter and husband."

Mrs. Garrett glared at Theodore, and he felt every bit the stranger in their home. "Dr. Cooper has seen me to wellness. I trust him to do the same for Rose."

Theodore's stomach was in knots and his chest was tight with barely contained frustration. He couldn't allow this, couldn't risk Rose to a charlatan. He wouldn't. He had to appeal his case, convince them.

But as he settled his gaze on Mrs. Garrett, he knew he had no choice.

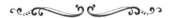

*September 21, 1918*
*Garrett Home*
*Mendota, IL*

So long Rose had only seen snatches of light. And even those were spaced far between. How long had she been in this place between light and dark? Only semi-conscious for pieces and parts.

In the midst, she wondered after her family. What had happened with them while this heavy sleep had weighed on her? And more...who was this man that kept coming and going on the edge of her awareness?

Was it Dr. Cooper? Or perhaps Theodore?

Why would Theodore be here? A part of her hoped he wasn't, while the better part of her craved for him to be by her bed when she found a way out of this haziness.

She was so close to the surface. Would she be able to break it?

Her body lay, disobedient and taxed by every small movement she attempted. But how else could she help herself arise?

After much effort, she opened her eyes. The world seemed blurry to her. Though each blink brought things into sharper focus.

It was night. Or was it? She couldn't be certain. The room was dark. Because someone had drawn the curtains? Or because it was night beyond the window?

She tried to move her head but only managed to shift slightly.

"Rose?" a masculine voice said from nearby. Movement belied that whomever it was moved even closer. "Rose, are you awake?"

The voice was all too familiar. And the part of her that wished for Theodore to be here rejoiced even as the other piece of her dismayed.

Turning in that direction, she could but see an outline. Maybe just a shadow of a dream?

The man reached toward the table by her head, and a lantern came to life. And she cringed against the assault on her senses. Although, little by little, she adjusted to it.

Warm hands captured one of hers. "Rose!"

The outline became detailed in the light. It was Theodore. His kind eyes appeared stormy almost. And his face was partially covered by a mask.

"Theodore?" Her voice was weak even to her ears. But she needed to reach out to him. Could he keep her from drowning again? "What...?"

He gripped her hand and set his other to her shoulder. "Do not trouble yourself. Take it slow."

She licked her lips, still they remained dry. As if she hadn't drunk in days.

"Here." He lifted her head and set a cup's rim to her mouth.

She drank, relishing the feel of the cool liquid.

When she finished, he laid her back down.

"No. I want to sit," came her protest. Far too long had she been caught in the netherworld. She wanted to bask in the light.

He helped her into a sitting position.

"How...?" She wasn't even sure what to ask. Where to start? "When...?"

"Easy. There will be plenty of time for everything to be answered."

She did so badly want to know all at once, but she sensed, too, that her body was frail and tired.

Her gaze wandered over the room. Father slept nearby in another bed, but her mother and brother were not in the room. Did that mean they had recovered?

"Where is my mother? And Silas?"

Theodore's tender gaze met hers. "They are well enough to have moved out of the sick room. They will be just fine."

She wanted to smile, but again, her body defied her. "More water."

He obliged and again helped her drink what she could manage.

"How long have I been in here?" The words were broken and labored, but she got them out.

"Over a week."

Her brows shot up. "A week?"

He nodded. "And then some."

Had he come at the behest of her family? Or Dr. Cooper? Or had he come of his own volition after hearing she was sick? "How...how long have you been here?"

"That whole time."

How was that possible?

"You came here to tend me?"

"How could I not come?"

Who notified him? And why?

He let out a breath and leaned forward a little more. "I took leave to come after your letters stopped. I arrived to find you quite unwell in the living room."

She had a rather hazy memory of being on the couch. Then of being carried. It was perhaps her last strong memory until now. "You...you brought me in here?"

"Yes." Something in his voice sounded edged. With frustration? Or was he somehow upset?

"And you've cared for me this whole time?"

"Yes. Well, myself and Clara. And Dr. Cooper." The way he said *Dr. Cooper* was definitely strained in some way. But she couldn't understand why. "I had my reservations about his ideas on managing this illness. Though I can't argue with his results...those ill in this home have recovered under his care."

"How is Clara?" She prayed her sister hadn't taken ill.

"She is well enough. She's just like her sister...caregiver at heart."

Rose did smile at that. Though how it came across to him, she couldn't be sure.

"And my father?" She glanced in the direction of his sleeping form again.

"He is on the mend. Well on his way to full health."

Her heart filled with gratitude. So much so it should burst. Her family was going to survive. How could she be more thankful?

Theodore interlaced their fingers. "I want you to rest now."

"No." Had she not slept enough? "I want to sit with you a bit longer."

"Then you'll rest?"

She gave a slight nod. "I promise."

"What else do you need to know?"

She wanted to ask for his thoughts on her family's home. Of her humble beginnings. "What did you tell my family? About us?"

"I told them we worked together. And that we had been exchanging letters."

"Oh." That didn't seem too committed. Had she thought more of their exchanges than he did? After all, he professed to love her.

"I didn't know quite what else to say. It's...difficult for me to put into words how I feel about you. How I have plans and dreams for a life with you."

She gasped. That was straightforward.

"But how do I say that to your parents, whom I just met? And all the while stealing you all from the grips of this plague?"

"You know I have hopes for us, too, right?"

The lines beside his eyes crinkled as if he smiled. "I do now."

"Now?" She didn't understand. Had her own profession of love for him not been enough?

"You...adamantly sought Dr. Cooper while ill. I had to wonder if you still felt for me the way you had before. Or if your affections had changed to make room for him."

"Dr. Cooper?" That didn't seem right. "Why would I have called for him?"

He shrugged dismissively. Almost as if he would rather forget the whole thing. "But you're awake now. I'm here. We can tell your family together."

"Tell them what?" She was tired, but still she needed him to say the words.

"That there is more ahead for us...together."

She relaxed into the smooth warmth of his voice and closed her eyes. There would be more to say, but she could rest in the fact that his intentions were for their life ahead.

"I think you'd best sleep now."

She wanted to argue, to insist they speak further. Yet the

fatigue clawed at her. If she refused would it drag her away from this moment? Dare she just surrender now?

He maneuvered her to a reclined position. Then his fingers were on the side of her face, caressing her. "Sleep well, my darling. I'll be here when you wake."

"Promise?"

"Of course." He continued to stroke her cheek.

And with the security of his watchfulness, she slipped into sleep.

## NINETEEN
# *darkness*

*May 10, 2020*
*Trammel Apartments*
*Cordova, TN*

S cott stared at the wall behind the loveseat. It was the same wall he had been staring at for the last hour. He had long since lost track of time. The sunlight on the wall had moved several inches.

What was he to do with himself? Alone in this apartment. He had been alone for days now. And would be for who knew how much longer.

Paul's admission to the hospital and worsening condition had given Scott reason to question his earlier stance on the information coming in. If Scott were to completely reject all news sources, there was precious little to go on.

Maybe, just maybe, there was some truth to the stats coming out. Perhaps not all of the advice and edicts were tainted by a political agenda. And, even if they were, there might still be some truth to be gleaned.

Could he trust part of the information and not the whole of it? Not throw the baby out with the bath water, as it were?

But what was real? What was conjecture? And what was straight up lies? It all seemed to blend together in his mind—both the things he had heard here and there and the concentrated research he had done these last couple of days.

With Paul regressing, Scott needed to occupy his mind and be more aware of what the chances were for his friend. As well as for himself.

The mandates didn't faze him as much. He had been careful when COVID had visited their apartment—cleaning the surfaces, wearing a mask when approaching Paul's room, and leaving his food and medicine at the door to that bedroom. He had not had contact with Paul in that time. Perhaps he would not get it.

But what if he did? What of that? And what if Paul died?

Around and around his thoughts swirled, circling back on themselves over and over again.

The isolation was getting to him.

He had taken a leave of absence from work as he found it quite impossible to dig into code while his friend lay in a hospital bed. And he had been helpless to stop it.

Brianne had tried to keep his spirits up, but it was for naught. He'd been ignoring her texts all day. And that wasn't like him. He knew that. He also knew she didn't deserve that.

But what did he have to offer anyone? He was empty. Completely empty.

As he let his mind wander, it drifted to the letters from the Spanish pandemic. His great grandfather had struggled with guilt when Rose got sick and it got him nowhere.

If Scott wasn't more mindful to aim his thoughts in a more positive direction, he feared he may fall into a dark place. Though he found he lacked the real care to direct his thoughts away from the truth.

Paul would likely die. And due to the contagious nature of the virus, Scott may follow him.

What was the point in fighting that truth?

The last call from Paul's mother had confirmed that he was now on a ventilator and had stopped responding. It looked grim.

Could Scott handle that? Losing his friend? Facing his own mortality?

He doubted he would be able to rise above.

So, he watched the wall.

The phone on the end table vibrated. He didn't bother looking at it. No doubt Brianne had tired of not having her texts returned. Or she was worried.

He didn't want to make her anxious after him. But he couldn't make himself answer the phone either. It would stop ringing. Eventually.

And it did.

Soon to be followed by a FaceTime ping.

That, too, would stop. In time.

Would she give up on him? Shouldn't she? Did he want her to?

Or did he no longer care?

So, he clicked his phone into silent mode and set it screen side down. There. Eventually, she would stop.

*May 10, 2020*
*Leyton Home*
*Bartlett, TN*

Brianne hung up her phone. Enough was enough. What was going on with Scott? Why wouldn't he answer her?

Something uneasy settled in her stomach, and she closed her eyes.

He must be greatly challenged. By the situation with Paul, the loneliness, all of it. And he was facing all of it without knowing who to trust in this whole politically charged mess.

She ached for his position. And she was mad at him. Then again, perhaps this was an echo of what he had gone through with her challenges.

Still, why would he shut her out? Of anyone on earth, why her? They were supposed to spend the rest of their lives together. Did he still want that?

She blew out a breath. This was not the time to let her emotions carry her away. Their relationship was solid. She *knew* Scott. And this was not like him.

Glancing at her car keys, she wondered. Should she check in on him? Would that be a big risk?

True, he wasn't out of quarantine, but he had not shown symptoms as of yesterday when last they spoke. And the chance of him having COVID decreased dramatically after the first three or four days. Or it seemed she remembered that being the case.

Mrs. Leyton's words about faith and trust came back to her.

Decision made, she grabbed her keys, mask, and purse.

"Latasha," she called as she stepped out of the guest room.

"Yeah?" came a voice from down the hall.

Brianne walked to Latasha's room and stopped in the doorway. "Scott still isn't answering."

Latasha frowned and then looked at Brianne's hands. "And you think you should go over there and check on him?"

Brianne chewed at her lip. Shouldn't she? "I...have to."

Latasha crossed the room to stand in front of Brianne. "Then don't let me stop you." A small smile crept onto Latasha's features.

Brianne nodded, relief rushing through her. "I'll need to isolate."

Latasha smirked. "You think that's what's going on here?"

"Not really. But I don't want to bring the coronavirus back here to your family."

Latasha thought for a moment. "We'll discuss that after. Just go."

Brianne touched her friend's arm. "Thank you."

Rushing from the house and to her car, she slid in and revved the engine.

Her phone buzzed. Scott?

Looking at the screen, she noted her sister's name. Had Dad gotten worse? Last she spoke with her mother, Dad had not had any bad symptoms. Just like a cold.

"Lori?" She breathed out as she answered.

"Hey! You sound winded. Everything okay?"

"Yeah. I'm just rushing a bit. Is everyone there okay?"

"For sure. Dad has never been better and Mom and I tested negative. I think we are over the worst of it here. How about Scott's roommate?"

Brianne hated to be the bearer of bad news. "They put him on a ventilator last week."

"Oh, I'm sorry to hear that. How is Scott?"

"As of yesterday, he was fine. A little down, but still symptom free."

"That's good news—wait, did you say yesterday?"

"Yeah. He hasn't returned my texts or answered my calls today." She hated to share so much with her sister. It wasn't her plan to make her family worry. But stuffing her own anxiety had never gotten her anywhere.

"Huh." Lori became quiet then.

"I'm about to go check on him."

"You think that's a good idea? What if he is sick?"

"I'll cross that bridge when...no *if* I come to it."

"Okay. I'll say a prayer for him."

"Thank you." She was getting more antsy by the second, so eager was she to get to Scott. "Gotta go, Lori. Talk later?"

"You'd better call me as soon as you can."

"Will do," Brianne promised before hanging up and tossing the phone into the passenger seat.

Shifting the car into reverse, she backed out of the driveway. Now she was a woman on a mission. Come what may.

*May 10, 2020*
*Trammel Apartments*
*Cordova, TN*

Knocking on the door woke Scott. When had he fallen asleep? He looked at his surroundings to try and catch his bearings. Deep sleep always did that to him.

He was in his apartment, on the couch in the living room. And he remembered watching the sunlight trace across the wall. As well as the dark thoughts.

Another knock, more insistent this time.

Who would be at his door? Everyone he knew understood that he was still quarantined for a couple more days.

Dragging himself to his feet, he shuffled across the living room.

"Who is it?" he managed, though maybe more biting than it should have been.

"Scott?"

Brianne? What was she doing here? She should stay far away,

safe. So stymied by her presence outside his apartment, he didn't respond.

"Scott, are you there?" Her words sounded desperate.

"Yes. I'm here. But I don't know that you should be." He stepped closer to the front door, but halted several paces away.

"I had to come. You weren't answering your phone."

He glanced at his phone, still screen side down on the end table.

"I got worried."

That tugged at his heart...she cared so much for him. And it flooded his heart with guilt. He should not have caused her to fret.

"Scott?"

"I'm here. I just...I'm sorry that I worried you."

"Can you open the door?" she called.

"I don't think that's a good idea." There was no chance he was risking her.

"I'll stay at least six feet away. I just want to see you and make sure you're okay."

He craved that, too. But would it be too difficult to see her and not be able to hold her? He needed that, too. That contact and that comfort.

"I'm not leaving until I see you."

She was willing to chance it for him? That was not the way she had handled the pandemic so far. What had changed?

"All right," he called. "I'm opening the door. Please, help me keep you safe."

"Okay." The word came out a bit confused. Did she not understand the extent to which he was drawn to her? Or how starved for contact he had become?

As he unlocked the door, he prayed for mindfulness to keep her at a distance. It was the first time he had prayed in days.

Swinging the door open, he drank in the sight of her. Though, he longed for a sweet smile instead of the mask that covered half her face.

"You don't look great." Her voice was painfully tender.

"Thanks." He chuckled. It felt good.

"Scott, I'm serious." Her brow furrowed.

"I'm still well enough. I just haven't exactly showered in a few days. Or attended to my hair. Who did I have to look good for?"

The edges of her eyes crinkled slightly as if she smiled.

A silence fell between them. She looked as if she were deep in thought, and he didn't have much to contribute, if anything.

"I'm sorry." Her voice wavered. And her eyes misted.

That was unexpected. "What?"

"I shut you out...in all the ways that mattered. And I was wrong to let this virus render me powerless to fear."

He frowned. That cut at him. Because he knew it was him now that did the pulling back.

"I could have been wise and cautious without sinking back into myself. That wasn't fair. I didn't trust God. And...I didn't trust you."

A thickness rose in his throat and he blinked back moisture. How could it be that her apology would so move him? Because she was dear to him. Because he loved her so fiercely.

And he had to hold onto that. It needed to drive him from the darkness and into the light. Could he, though?

"It's all right, Brie. This has been...impossibly difficult to navigate." He paused, biting at his lower lip for a second. "For both of us."

She watched him as a tear made its way down her face.

"I did my fair share of trying to get through this on my own." Even now, he knew the path forward, but did he have the strength to take it? Not on his own.

"We can get through this...together. As long as we have a solid foundation."

How did she become so wise? She was right. They couldn't do it on their own. Only by relying on God.

*But...* His mind whispered at him. *What if Paul dies? What then? How can you believe God is good?*

He closed his eyes and worked to push that thought to the side.

"What is it?" came Brianne's gentle voice.

Dare he tell her his worst fear? But he knew...it was only powerful against him in the dark. If he were able to shine light on the thoughts, they would lose their hold.

"I worry about Paul. I worry about me getting sick."

She nodded. "I know. And that is fair. But we can't stop living because of what might happen. That's something I'm beginning to realize. I've done that for so long."

Once more, he just took her in. All of her. She looked well and at peace. For the first time in months.

And he wanted that for himself. And for her.

But could he surrender to God's plan? There were too many 'ifs' in this whole situation.

*Blessed are those who have not seen and yet have believed.*

Yes, he had to take the step lit in front of him. Even though the path was not yet illuminated. He had to trust that God would care for his footfalls and guide him...even if only one step at a time. "Pray with me?"

She just looked at him. At first, he feared she had not heard him.

Then she smiled. "Always."

# TWENTY

*September 27, 1918*
*Garrett Home*
*Mendota, IL*

Rose had worked diligently to regain her strength and then no one could hold her back. She returned to caring for the family.

She heated some water for tea and wiped down the counter. The urge to clean every square inch of the house was one she had to temper. For she did not have her full stamina back. But she did what she could to avoid sitting down and being cornered by Theodore. Why, she wasn't sure.

Letting out a slow breath, she poured hot water over her tea bag in a mug. She was alone right now. Maybe she could sit for a minute. What was Theodore doing, after all?

She settled at the dining table and sipped the warm liquid.

"Rose?"

Sputtering, she nearly spit out what was in her mouth.

She turned.

Theodore stood in the doorway to the kitchen.

"Yes?" She wiped at her mouth, hoping she hadn't made too much of a fool of herself.

"I was just looking for you." He stepped within and took the seat across from her. "It seems you hardly sit still these days."

She nodded and lifted the cup to her lips again. Hopefully she wouldn't have to respond just yet.

"I, ah, received word from my commanding officer."

Oh no. She may not be ready to chat with him, but that didn't mean she wanted him to leave.

"He insists I return. The numbers are bad, Rose. Sickness is killing more people than the war."

Her eyes widened. "You can't mean that."

He nodded but looked grim. "I do. The statistics coming from all fronts are indicating that. Though, it may not all be attributed to the Spanish flu. You know what those trenches and frontline conditions can be like. It's not surprising soldiers are getting sick. But this flu is wiping out civilians, too. It's not looking good."

She swallowed hard.

"And they need me back at my post."

Staring at him, she couldn't seem to make her mouth work. It was a lot.

His eyebrows met and lowered. He didn't look happy. Was he waiting on her to speak? "I suppose I'll get my things together."

"Wait." She set a hand to his arm. "I..."

"What?"

"I don't want you to go."

He looked at her hand, pale against the more tan complexion of his arm. "I can't pretend I haven't noticed you avoiding me. What I don't understand is why."

She looked down, chewing at her lip. "I don't really know."

"Just a few days ago, we were speaking words of the future. Then you shut me out."

She nodded. How could she deny it? "I...just feel so uneven."

"Uneven?"

She hugged herself, rubbing hands up and down her arms. "I don't know. Things with you are one way. And then there's my family."

"I'm not sure what you mean to say."

She sighed, standing and moving to the sink. "I feel so..." How could she say it? "There's a reason I wasn't forthcoming about my family before."

He stood but remained by the table. "What do you mean? Your family is wonderful."

"I know. It's just...you came from a more affluent situation. I didn't want you to think less of me because of this." She waved a hand as if to encompass the whole house.

He took a step closer. "You think that matters to me?"

She sniffled and looked at the floor.

"That's what you think of me? That I'm so caught up in money and comfortable living that I would abandon you?"

It sounded bad when he said it.

"I don't think that about you," she insisted. But her words rang hollow in light of the truth. "I don't know what I was thinking."

"Seems like it's more about what you think of your family."

She speared him with a look. "That's not fair. I love my family."

"I'm sure you do. Are you not satisfied with humble beginnings?"

"I don't know." She looked out the nearby window. "How could I not be satisfied? My parents did everything to see to our comfort and to get me to nursing school."

"That's the kind of parents they are. They want to help your dreams come true."

How was it he knew her parents so well? Saw things it had taken her years to come to terms with?

"I just...don't know what to say. I was so wrong."

He strode to where she remained and set hands on her arms. "They are the kind of parents I hope we are someday." Reaching up, he tucked a strand of hair behind her ear.

That brought a smile to her face. "Really?"

"In fact, I was...hoping we might make our situation official." He waggled his eyebrows. It was comical.

"Truly?"

"I love you, Rose. And I am decided on this: I want to spend the rest of my life loving you." He leaned in, his lips a breath away from hers.

She lifted her hands to settle on his shoulders. "Then I'm not letting you get away."

His mouth pressed to hers and they sealed their plans with their lips and with their hearts.

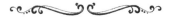

*September 30, 1918*
*Justice of the Peace*
*Mendota, IL*

Theodore gripped Rose's hand as they ascended the few steps into the courthouse. This was it. He and Rose would walk in as two individuals. And walk out joined in matrimony.

The road to this day had not been terribly long...yet it had been so painstakingly difficult. With the war ongoing and the flu taking lives by the hundreds, he was glad they could take the happiness that was offered them by God. For this moment. For this day.

Her father had given Theodore his blessing, but it was only he and Rose that made this trip.

She wore her mother's best outfit for church and a smile on her face.

Perhaps Clara would wear the same smile when she married Dr. Cooper later this month. Surely Theodore's jealousy had blinded him to what was really going on. Feelings had developed between Clara and the doctor. Slowly, and over the strain of the pandemic. Something he and Rose knew all about.

But in a month, the Garrett family would have certainly gotten bigger.

He wouldn't be opposed to adding to that number with Rose sooner rather than later. When the Spanish flu had run its course in the world. And not a moment before.

And even if it didn't come to an end, he would love Rose and hold her close for the days they were given.

"Ready?" he said, turning toward her as he halted to let her take a breath. In his eagerness, he had forgotten to pace himself for her benefit.

"Absolutely." She squeezed his hand. "You?"

"Never been more ready for anything in my life." He leaned toward her and pressed a kiss to the side of her face. "Now, let's get in there so the next kiss will be for my wife.

# TWENTY-ONE

## *found*

*May 20, 2020*
*Leyton Home*
*Bartlett, TN*

Brianne clutched her phone to herself. This was pure torture. Yesterday made fourteen days post exposure for Scott. And today he would officially be finished with quarantine. She ached to touch him, to hold him. Then they could begin putting this nightmare behind them.

His spirit had lifted considerably and his mood had brightened. Seemed they both had some growing to do in their ability to trust God. But Brianne no longer wondered about His faithfulness. He was true to word. And He was good. He had walked with her and Scott through hardship. Even if things didn't go the way she wanted them to.

A small knock on the guest room door jerked her attention from her silent phone.

"Come in," she called.

The door opened and Latasha stood just on the other side. "Any word yet?"

"No. Nothing."

"Why don't we go on a little walk down the neighborhood nature trail?" She smiled. Was she sympathetic to Brianne's plight? "It'll help take your mind off it."

"But I could be out there when he calls."

"So? You can still get to your car just fine. Besides, some fresh air and exercise never hurt anyone."

Brianne grinned. She was right. They had taken to walking around the neighborhood of late. It always bolstered Brianne's spirits. Maybe she was, in fact, solar powered.

"All right. But I'm not responsible if I leave you in my dust when Scott calls."

Latasha held up her hands in surrender. "Fine, fine."

Brianne reached for her sneakers and made quick work of lacing them. Then she glanced at her light jacket. "Is it chilly outside?"

"Not at all. It's beautiful."

Brianne nodded and followed her out of the house and down the road to where the trail picked up. They had yet to venture onto this carved out path, but had every intention. So, if nothing else, this marked one thing off their list.

As they walked, they made easy conversation. Latasha had always been good about that. They moved into a more densely forested area. How much longer did the trail go?

"We're almost to the end." Latasha seemed to have read her mind. "Then we'll turn around. I promise."

Brianne pulled out her phone.

"What are you doing?"

"Just checking." She flashed Latasha a smile. Hopefully one that got her out of trouble. "I just can't stand the waiting."

Then Latasha's feet seemed to sweep out from under her.

"Are you okay?" Brianne turned to see her friend on the ground.

Latasha sat up. "Yeah. I'm fine." She brushed the dirt off her shirt and pants. "But I may need a minute."

Brianne looked back the way they had come. "Should I go get Donnelle? Or your dad?"

"No way," Latasha's response was almost biting. "I'll manage. Just give me a minute to rest my foot. I think I tripped on a root or something."

Brianne scanned the ground. The path was littered with sticks and other miscellaneous things. It could have been anything.

"Why don't you finish the trail? It ends just around that bend. Then I'll join you on your way back to the house. I should have collected my breath by then."

Brianne didn't feel right about leaving Latasha there on the ground. Certainly not walking off. "I'd rather stay with you. Unless we need to go for help."

"Nonsense." Latasha looked around. "Just help me to that bench. I'll be fine until you get back. I have my phone on me. It's all good. I promise."

Brianne supported Latasha as she stood and then hobbled to the bench. "Really, I don't mind sitting with you until you're ready to head back."

"Can I honestly not get rid of you? I just need a minute *to myself* to catch my breath."

Is that how it was then? Latasha needed to be alone to get out whatever pent-up frustration welled under the surface. Did she just want Brianne out of earshot?

"Okay. But if the path goes much farther, I won't go the whole way."

"Fair enough." Latasha rubbed her ankle. "Now, go, leave me be."

Guilt stuck in Brianne's chest and squeezed. But what could

she do? Latasha wanted a minute. Maybe she could just go around the bend and wait there, well within earshot. Yes, that would make Latasha feel better.

"All right. Call for me if you need anything." She moved off toward the bend and resisted the urge to keep looking over her shoulder. That would not make Latasha happy. Was Brianne turning into a mother hen?

She rounded the bend and prepared to stop when she spotted a figure ahead on the pathway. Someone else taking a stroll? Maybe she should go back to Latasha in case there was trouble.

The figure walked her way.

Was she in danger?

She prepared to run back to Latasha when the man's gait caught her attention. Was that...?

Frozen to the spot, she couldn't speak as Scott moved closer.

How did he get here? Why hadn't he called her? What were the chances she'd come across him on this trail?

Then she realized. This was all a ruse.

"Scott?" she called, wanting to confirm with her ears what her heart knew.

He picked up the pace, as did she, and in a moment they rushed into each other's embrace.

She clung to him as if never to let go. Indeed, she hoped not to.

He pressed kisses to her hair, to her face, and lastly to her lips.

It felt so good to be in his arms. Nothing had ever felt so much like home.

When he pulled back, he set his hands to her face. "You're real. You're here...like, in person."

She teared up. "I could say the same about you."

He pressed his face into her shoulder and drew her close again. "What do you say...will you still marry me?"

She released a breath that had been pent up for months. "Yes. Here, now, wherever, whenever..."

He laughed. "I love you, Brie."

"And I love you. So much."

So long they had been separated by the virus and by fear. No longer. And she rejoiced silently that she was whole again. With him.

*June 15, 2020*
*Shelby Farms Park*
*Memphis, TN*

Scott watched as Brianne pushed the last bite of sandwich into her mouth. The peaceful surroundings of the park's picnic area was absolutely perfect today.

Brianne fairly shone. A smile every now and again, a light-hearted laugh, and her hair was radiant in the sunlight.

She glanced at him. "What?"

Or that's what the word sounded like. It was difficult to discern through her full mouth.

"Didn't your mother ever tell you not to talk with food in your mouth?"

She smirked but finished the bite before continuing. "Didn't your mother ever tell you it's not polite to stare?"

He laughed and leaned in for a kiss.

When they parted, she said, "Hey..."

"Yeah?"

"I have something for you." She reached into her tote bag and pulled out his great grandparents' letters.

He accepted them into his grasp.

"They really were a wonderful thing these last weeks. I'm sorry that we didn't read them together."

He nodded. "I'm glad that you liked them." Then he swallowed. "I wish I could have known them."

"I wonder what they would have thought of the coronavirus pandemic."

"Our leaders certainly reacted differently."

"The world is different. We're not in the midst of the war to end all wars," Brianne pointed out.

"I also wonder what they'd think of me. And you."

"Oh, for certain, they'd be proud of you. Look at you...a well accomplished programmer, respected in your field."

He shook his head and looked at the wooden table top.

"You are a kind, generous, servant-hearted man."

He glanced back up at her. The sincerity in her eyes took his breath.

"And you are loved by all who know you."

He pressed another kiss to the side of her face. "Not to mention, I have the most amazing woman to do life with."

She blushed. "I love that you see the best in me."

"I love that you see the real me," he countered. "And love me just the same."

"Awww...stop."

He took her hand in his and dropped his voice a bit. "Did you ever think it could be so good?"

She leaned into him. "Never."

He wanted to lose himself in her gentle embrace for a time. But they had some things to hash out. "I hate to change the subject, but Rochelle from Cherry Lane Inn called again."

"Oh?" Brianne grabbed for a cluster of grapes. "What did you tell her?"

"That I couldn't wait to marry you." He grinned.

She swatted at him. "Be serious."

"I am. That's what I told her. And she completely understood.

They still aren't able to host full wedding events yet anyway. We'll be able to get our deposit back."

"Great."

"Are you sure you want to go ahead? We could have that big wedding in six months perhaps."

"Are you kidding?" She snared his arm with hers. "If I've learned anything this last year, it's to take hold of the opportunities as they come. And that we are stronger together than apart."

He nodded. "I just don't want you to regret anything about our wedding."

"Regret anything? How could I? It's you and me...together...for the rest of our lives."

He loved her for that...among so many other reasons.

"Will Paul be able to stand up with you at the wedding?"

Scott was so thankful his friend was alive and well. He almost wasn't. Paul had come to the brink. And back. But that didn't mean he didn't have long term effects. "He will be lugging an oxygen tank most certainly, and might be in a wheelchair, but he is still excited to be my best man."

"If we need to wait until he's better..."

"Oh no. You're not getting away that easily." He wrapped his arms around her.

She accepted his kiss and his embrace.

He basked in her unabashed display of affection. And cherished it.

For the future was theirs.


*Keep reading for a sneak peek of the first book in the Convenient Risk Series!*

*Thank you, dear reader, for for reading along with me! If you enjoyed this story, I would sincerely appreciate if you would submit a review. It would mean so much to me!*

**To read more about these characters, follow along with the Across the Years Series. Find it at:**

https://saraturnquist.com/across-the-years-series/

# author's note

This is a book of my heart for certain. And it was difficult to write at times. But it needed to be written.

I struggled, as you may have, dear reader, with the lack of progress Theodore was able to make on his research. I wish this was a happier story. But it is what it is. So much of what science and medicine knew and discovered during the Spanish flu pandemic amounted to less than hoped for. In a lot of ways, they were simply on the wrong track. For at that time, it was believed the flu was caused by a bacteria. This, of course, would set researchers on a wrong path as it is a viral infection. The absence of antibiotics in the early 1900s also contributed to a lack of care. As many infected with the Spanish flu (a H1N1 flu virus) would die from secondary pneumonias and other bacterial infections.

It wasn't until the 1950s and 1960s that any real progress was made to identify the virus and begin to suppose how treatments may have made a difference.

One of the more interesting things about the Spanish flu was how quickly it killed. A person would wake up coughing and have passed by the evening. It didn't always kill so swiftly, but it did.

Also, the fact that it tended to strike individuals in their 20s-40s the hardest. Which is contradictory to everything known about illnesses at the time. Many scientists believe the Spanish flu virus created what's called a cytokine storm...whereas the immune system, which produces cytokines as a part of its natural functions, would attack the individuals internal organs. This would have, of course, exacerbated the illness, if not directly leading to the death of the person.

So many similarities exist between the Spanish flu pandemic and the COVID-19 pandemic. But there are great differences as well. Being more aware and informed, a double-edged sword even as it could be, helped reduce the spread. During the 1920s, there was no such thing as sick pay. So you can imagine how one would go to work, though sick, in order to support the family. And factories at this time were poorly ventilated and crowded, only enhancing the virus's ability to spread. Likewise, the movement of soldiers across the globe for the war effort, as well as huddling in camps and trenches with already less than ideal conditions, aided the spread.

In the end, the Spanish flu would have three waves. The first, while deadly, did not compare to the others. More people would succumb to the Spanish flu than the number that died in the entire World War. It was just mind boggling how many fell to this pandemic.

Overall, I pray that we have learned to be kinder to those suffering - whether that is physically or psychologically, as there have been many who have fought on both fronts.

Amanda stared at the blood on her hands. Her husband's blood. She was numb. Cried out. She shoved the door open with her hip and stepped into the fading day. Her focus was on the water pump across the yard. The few steps stretched out before her. Holding her hands away from her body, she moved toward it, not caring that she stirred the dust of the dry earth beneath her feet.

The pump's handle was solid and cold. She yanked her hand back. Jed's blood now stained the metal. It couldn't be helped. Grasping the handle once more, she pulled it up then pressed down. Her long blonde hair fell into her face. Amanda fought the urge to push it to the side. Again and again she pumped, until water began to flow from the spout. Thrusting her hands underneath, she rubbed at the dark red covering her skin.

Once all traces were gone, she tugged at her apron, wrapping her hands in the thin fabric. When she looked at them again, they shook. And she could still see the deep crimson upon them.

She blinked. The red vanished.

Spinning on the balls of her feet, she turned back toward the house. The clicking of her shoes alerted her that she was once again inside.

And the smell.

"Where were you?" A gruff voice greeted her.

She jerked in that direction.

The tall frame of the doctor filled the doorway to her bedroom. His scowl accused her.

"I needed some fresh air."

He shook his head. Had she disappointed him? "You were needed in here."

She nodded, lowering her gaze to the floor as she stepped toward him.

He held up his hands. "There's no point now. He's passed."

"What?" It wasn't possible.

The doctor moved past her, his shoulder grazing hers. "It was only a matter of time."

Amanda's heart stopped. Cold surrounded and pervaded her being. Her breath rushed out of her. Would she be able to draw in another?

In time, it did come, but with it came the tears. There were more. After all.

### To read more, find *A Convenient Risk* here:

https://saraturnquist.com/convenient-risk/

**Read the rest of the ACROSS THE YEARS Series!**

# Among the Pages (Book 1)

### A woman's choice...is in question.

Brianne finds the diary of a distant relative, and she is drawn into the story of Margaret, a passionate woman in 1915 who seems to whisper from the past.

And so, Brianne is whisked along as Margaret joins the fight for women's rights. Before long, things spin out of control. Will she land on her feet? Or be forever lost to herself?

*Will she land on her feet? Or be forever lost to herself?*

# Between the Lines (Book 2)

### A couple's hope for the future is in peril... until they find connection in the past.

Scott and Brianne are ready to step into their happily ever after. They are counting down the days 'til they wed...until COVID-19 upends everything they have planned.

Scott receives his great grandparents' letters to each other in the midst of the 1920s Spanish flu pandemic when their romance blossoms despite the overwhelming fear and sadness that surrounds them.

**What will Scott and Brianne glean from the past? And how will they face down the struggles rampant in a worldwide crisis?**

*acknowledgments*

First, for those who read my work as it is produced - Kelly Holloman, Cindy Smith, and my sweet husband - you are truly sent from heaven. It helps the direction of the story and my confidence to continue.

My craft partner, Kelly Hollman...I cannot thank you enough for your unending support and spot on feedback. You are amazing!

To my editor, Julie Sherwood, thank you for making my words sing.

Cora Graphics, you've put out another cover that amazes me!

To Becky Brabham, you lend your talent and your voice to my characters...making them more real.

My friends and family, your support cannot be overstated. I love you all so very much!

*about the author*

Sara is a coffee lovin', word slinging, Historical Romance author whose super power is converting caffeine into novels. She loves those odd little tidbits of history that are stranger than fiction. That's what inspires her. Well, that and a good love story.

But of all the love stories she knows, hers is her favorite. She lives happily with her own Prince Charming and their gaggle of minions. Three to be exact. They sure know how to distract a writer! But, alas, the stories must be written, even if it must happen in the wee hours of the morning.

Sara is an avid reader and enjoys reading and writing clean Historical Romance when she's not traveling.

Please follow along with her journey through her newsletter at:
http://saraturnquist.com/list

**Happy Reading!**

facebook.com/AuthorSaraRTurnquist

instagram.com/sararturnquist

x.com/sararturnquist

youtube.com/@SaraRTurnquist

pinterest.com/sararturnquist

# also by sara r. turnquist

## CONVENIENT RISK SERIES

*A Convenient Risk*

*An Inconvenient Christmas*

*A Less Convenient Path*

*A Convenient Escape*

*An Inconvenient Acquaintance*

*These Golden Years*

*A Less Convenient Arrangement*

*Ranch Hands Collection* (ebook only)

## CRIPPLE CREEK SERIES

*Hope in Cripple Creek*

*Christmas in Cripple Creek*

*Faith in Cripple Creek*

*Love in Cripple Creek*

*~ Prequels ~*

*Leaving Waverly*

*Leaving Stoneybrook*

## LADY OF BOHEMIA SERIES

*The Lady Bornekova*

*The Lady and the Hussites*

*The Lady and Her Champion*

*The Lady and Her Secret*

**RAILWAY ROMANCE SERIES**

*Laura, The Tycoon's Daughter*

**STANDALONE NOVELS**

*The General's Wife*

*Trail of Fears*

*Off to War*